An Unhappy Medium

DAWN EASTMAN

BERKLEY PRIME CRIME, NEW YORK

BERKLEY PRIME CRIME

**An imprint of Penguin Random House LLC
375 Hudson Street, New York, New York 10014**

AN UNHAPPY MEDIUM

A Berkley Prime Crime Book / published by arrangement with the author

ISBN: 978-0-425-28280-9

PUBLISHING HISTORY
Berkley Prime Crime mass-market edition / April 2016

PRINTED IN THE UNITED STATES OF AMERICA

10 9 8 7 6 5 4 3 2 1

Cover illustration by Daniel Craig.
Cover design by Judith Lagerman.
Design element: iStockphoto/Thinkstock.

Penguin
Random
House

To my most avid readers, Ann and Bob Eastman.

Acknowledgments

Thank you to all the readers who have embraced the Fortune family. Clyde and the gang would still be rattling around in my head if not for your enthusiasm and support.

Thank you to my editor, Katherine Pelz, and the entire Berkley team. It takes a village to bring Crystal Haven to readers.

Thanks go to my agent, Sharon Bowers, for supporting the series from the beginning.

I will always be grateful for my writing group, Wendy Delsol, Kim Stuart, Kali Van Baale, and Carol Spaulding for their investment and dedication to these characters.

And, as always, thanks to my family—Steve, Jake, and Ellie—who have grown accustomed to discussing murder and mayhem anytime, anywhere.

1

My chest burned, my legs ached, and I felt a cramp in the vicinity of my liver. The raspy breaths behind me spurred me forward. My own breathing came in harsh gasps but I knew I couldn't stop. I wouldn't let him catch me.

"Clyde, stop."

I continued running, but felt my pace slip. I couldn't keep this up, but I refused to let him win. He was right behind me.

"You're going to hurt yourself," he said.

I slowed and turned toward my nephew, Seth, who was jogging in place and grinning broadly. Tuffy, Seth's shih tzu, panted heavily while looking adoringly up at his boy. Baxter, my bullmastiff running partner, sighed and leaned against my leg. I received no adoring looks.

I felt my eyes narrow and I would have turned and sprinted on if it weren't for the wave of nausea that overtook me at the thought of running any farther. It was Seth's fault I stood here in the first place.

Running. I hated it. I had done it out of necessity during police training and then had continued in a haphazard way just to stay fit enough to chase criminals, who, fortunately, were often overweight and out of shape. But I hadn't chased a criminal in a year and I hadn't missed it. I'd also slacked off on the cardio, and mooched rich, carb-heavy dinners at my mom's house too often, much to my current dismay.

Seth and my friend Alex had decided to sponsor a Zombie Apocalypse Fun Run and give the proceeds to the Ottawa County animal rescue league. I wasn't having fun yet. But, it was a worthy cause and the only reason I was back out on the pavement running in circles around Crystal Haven. The Fun Run was scheduled for Friday. Two days away. Between studying for my private investigator's license, fending off my aunt's business proposals, and utilizing my world-class avoidance skills, I had put off training. My mistake had been to run with Seth. His fourteen years to my thirty was an advantage I had initially ignored. My innate competitiveness had forced me to try to outrun him.

"Okay, you go on ahead." I continued to gulp air and waved him forward. "I'll just head back to the house with Tuffy—he looks like he could use a drink."

Seth barely hid his smile, but I was too relieved to call him on it. We traded leashes and he and Baxter loped off at an easy pace while I hobbled home with Tuffy. It was unusual for the shih tzu and I to be paired up. Tuffy was Seth's dog and Baxter was mine, but in this case the little guy was the better partner for me. He glanced up at me with a scowl that seemed to say, "Why did I have to get involved in this?"

"Don't look at me, he's your boy," I said.

Tuffy sniffed loudly and looked away.

I said, "Let's go get a treat." He perked up enough to trot back home, his tail curled jauntily over his back. It was a pleasant walk now that winter had finally moved on and spring buds showed bright green. My neighborhood was a tree-lined mix of Victorians, Craftsmans, bungalows, and log cabins. All was quiet on this Wednesday morning, but by the weekend it would be alive with kids, dogs, bikers, and gardeners.

We turned the corner and I saw my mom's orange smart car parked in the street outside my house. I slowed my pace. Mom dropping by unexpectedly and waiting for me did not bode well. Tuffy also sensed we had a visitor, and pulled on the leash to hurry me along.

Mom and Aunt Vi sat on my porch in the wicker chairs I had just brought out of winter storage. Aunt Vi stopping by usually meant she had another job for me to do for "our" new business. The psychic finding business was Vi's idea. It consisted of my aunt collecting clients and promising I would solve their problems. Vi stood as we approached.

Her usual outfit of long black skirt, jewel-toned top, and cardigans had morphed to a multicolored skirt and top in bright spring colors with the change of season. She had also lost a couple of layers of cardigan in deference to the warmer temperatures. Her long gray hair was braided to the side and hung over her right shoulder.

"I knew it!" she said. "I knew you should be on a zombie team instead of a running team. You need to sit down."

Vi took Tuffy's leash from me.

I grimaced at her, but didn't argue.

The Fun Run was arranged such that the runners were in teams to protect each other from the zombies that would be scattered in groups throughout the course. Vi had gleefully volunteered to be a zombie leader and had been studying makeup techniques on the Internet for weeks. I thought again that I should have been training for weeks, or months, and now I regretted not listening to Vi.

"Are you sure you feel okay?" Mom said. She regarded me carefully as I sat on the top porch step.

"She looks overheated," Vi said.

"Hmm," Mom said. She tilted her head at me and *tsk*ed. "She's going to have a rough time this weekend."

"Sitting right here, folks," I said.

They exchanged one of their looks and Mom changed tactics.

"We have some great news! Let's go inside," Mom said. She stood and took Tuffy's leash from Vi. Mom was stunning in a completely different way from her sister. Her silver hair was pulled back into a neat chignon, her makeup was flawless, and she wore chinos, a silk blouse, and short blazer. "You look like you need some water," she said to the dog.

We trooped into my living room and Mom released Tuffy from his leash. He dashed toward the kitchen and I heard him slurping water from his bowl and probably onto the floor.

"What's the good news?" I asked, secretly hoping that the run had been canceled.

"Grace, Paul, and Sophie are coming to visit!" Mom said. She clasped her hands under her chin and grinned, but it didn't fool me. Grace, my sister, and her husband, Paul, had not been to Crystal Haven in fifteen years. They lived in New York City and both worked for an investment firm there. Recently, Seth had come to live with me due to a desire to get out of the city and his vague sense that his parents were in some sort of trouble.

They had never shown the slightest interest in coming to Crystal Haven, opting to send Seth and his sister, Sophie, for unaccompanied summer visits. It was one of those things we never talked about in my family. I had been devastated when my big sister left, and although my parents were pleasant when they visited New York, the warmth that I remembered wasn't there. We all loved the kids and their visits were the highlight of every summer for my parents. But the only time we had all been together was on a few holidays in New York. I quickly sat on the couch and tried to stop my mind from formulating a list of the reasons Grace might want to come to Michigan. None of them were good. I uncharitably wondered what kind of trouble she was trying to stir up. However, she probably wanted to see Seth. He had been talking up this Fun Run for months. I convinced myself she was just being a supportive parent.

I tried to ignore the tightening in my gut that told me something else was going on.

"You can't tell Seth," Vi said. "They want to surprise him."

"The cards told me that the zombie run would be full of excitement," Mom said. "But I had no idea what that meant until they called from the airport to say they were on their way."

Mom is a tarot card reader by profession and tends to consult the cards for everything from what to have for dinner to whether there is danger lurking in the murky future. I used to bristle at this obsession with tarot cards and guarding against impending dangers, but last fall I learned that Mom had been given a disturbing prediction that she would attend the funeral for one of her children. I tended to cut her some slack now, knowing that she absolutely believed she would outlive either my sister or me.

"We aren't telling your father, either," Vi said. "He can't keep a secret to save his life." She waved her hand dismissively.

I thought this was unfair, but sometimes it was better to ignore Vi rather than argue.

"Okay," I said. I glanced at Tuffy and narrowed my eyes at him. I wasn't sure how much the little dog understood. Vi claims to be a pet psychic, and if her bank account is anything to go by, a lot of people believe her. I'm on the fence, myself. However, Seth really *can* communicate with animals and if Tuffy revealed this secret, I was surely the one they would blame. Seth wasn't ready to reveal his talent to the rest of the family and I was the only one who knew about his Dr. Doolittle tendencies.

It might seem that these are unusual career choices, but in Crystal Haven, those with psychic talent vastly outnumber those without. We offer everything from tarot to séances, crystals to palm reading, as well as some herbal medicines, potions, and spell kits. The town could have survived as a tourist destination on location alone, but the psychic offerings meant we had a bit of an edge, for the right person, over other small towns along the coast of Lake Michigan. I had run from Crystal Haven and my own psychic talent, but after almost a year back in my hometown, I was glad I had returned.

"When are they arriving?" I asked.

"Later this afternoon," Mom said. "She thought they would be here in time for dinner. I know it's more of a winter dish, but I'm going to make pot roast. It was always her favorite growing up."

Mom glanced at her watch and tugged on Vi's sleeve.

"We should go," Mom said. "I have to get to the store or we won't eat until nine o'clock tonight."

"You and Seth need to come for dinner," Vi said. "But don't tell him anything. Bring Mac." She paused, and tilted her head. "You can probably tell him if you want. He seems pretty good at secrets."

Vi was still irked with Mac, my boyfriend, for not including her in a recent murder investigation. He's a homicide detective for Ottawa County and had moved back to the area around the same time I had. Mom called it fate, Vi called it destiny, I called it amazing.

After several murders over the past year that frequently had us working at cross purposes, I was looking forward to a leisurely summer spending time with Mac. I hoped that would happen after the Zombie Apocalypse Fun Run. This was also Founder's Day weekend and the official kickoff of the summer tourist season. Mac and I planned to skip the reenactment, wander through the food tents, and enjoy the bonfire.

I waved my mom and Vi out the door and took a deep breath. I still had that clenched feeling deep inside. I leaned against the door and closed my eyes. I had been working with an old friend of my grandmother's, Neila Whittle, to hone my own psychic skills. I am able to find lost objects, can often sense good (or bad) intentions, have dreams of doom, and gut feelings that never seem specific enough to actually help. I was tired of ignoring the flashes of insight I received unbidden. She was helping me to learn how to interpret and even encourage the information.

This time, however, I wasn't able to calm the swirling thoughts and vague unease. I pushed off from the door and headed up the stairs for a quick shower.

I would go see Neila before my sister's plane touched down in Michigan.

2

I had passed Seth on my way out the door, telling him the dinner plan and casting what I hoped was a threatening glance at Tuffy.

My ancient Jeep groaned a bit as I turned onto a steep driveway that appeared to lead straight into the woods. Bumping upward through oak and maple trees budding with leaves, I rolled down the window to inhale the scent of pine and fresh air. We had survived a brutal winter with more than the usual amount of snow and cold. I had promised myself I would enjoy the good weather once it arrived.

Neila's house looked the same as ever. Tucked among the trees and covered in vines such that it appeared to have grown right out of the woods, it looked deserted and possibly haunted. It was an impression that the reclusive owner did not try to alter. Neila was just as happy to be left alone in her small clearing in the pines. A few changes had been made since the first time I had driven up here last fall. Motion-activated floodlights now glowered from the corners of the house, the sagging stoop had been repaired, and the shutters currently hung straight. Neila had grown too old to deal with teenage thrill seekers, and a friend had helped her with repairs.

Keeping secrets ran in my family, and my mother didn't know I had been visiting Neila regularly. Neila had an unusual psychic talent. She knew when a parent was going to lose a child. I shivered every time I thought of it. She was the source of my mother's free-floating fear. I had kept my visits and my knowledge about the prediction from my mother, at least so far.

The door swung slowly open on creaky hinges as I stepped onto the small porch.

"Clytemnestra, it's so good to see you," Neila said. She pulled the door wide and I bent to hug the tiny woman dressed in a long gray dress and shawl. She *also* appeared to have sprung from the forest itself, an elderly woodland creature. She was one of the few people who got away with using my full name.

"Hello, Neila," I said.

"Have I lost track of the days again?" she asked. "I didn't expect you today."

I shook my head and smiled. "No, this is a surprise visit."

"Oh, good." She splayed her hand across her chest. "Come to the back and we'll have some tea. You can tell me what's got you all knotted up." She swung her arm toward a dark hallway that I knew led to the large cozy kitchen at the back of the house.

I settled myself in my usual spot at the table and she poured tea into a dainty teacup. She pushed a plate of cookies in my direction and I couldn't help thinking I hadn't surprised her at all.

I glanced around the room I had come to love. An enormous fireplace dominated one wall with what could only be called a cauldron hanging on a rack over the fire. The walls were stone, lending an ancient feel to the room. The opposite wall held a modern fridge, stove, and micro-wave, but I knew she preferred to use the fireplace for things like stew and potions.

"So, tell me," she said after watching me eat a cookie.

"Grace is coming to town today," I said.

She took a deep breath and let it out. "Ah."

"I don't know why I have this sense of dread, but I can't seem to shake it. The moment I heard she was coming I felt . . . anxious. She's been away a long time and I'm sure there will be drama—there always is with Grace. But this is something more."

Neila nodded and drummed her fingers on the table. She sat back and put her hands in her lap, closing her eyes. After a few moments she opened them and shook her head.

"I'm not sensing anything," she said. "Are you sure this has to do with your sister and not something else?"

"I think so." I took another sip of tea and set the cup in its saucer. "It started as soon as Mom told me she was coming."

"You didn't feel anything before that?" Neila rested

her elbows on the table and leaned forward, pulling her shawls tighter across her shoulders.

"I've been worried about this weekend for a while now, but that's because I signed up to participate in this crazy zombie run Seth and Alex are organizing." I broke off a piece of cookie. "I'm not excited about it." That was an understatement.

"Maybe your feelings have nothing to do with the running."

I considered that. She could be right. Even with all the work I had done with her over the past few months, I was still not adept at interpreting the messages I received. So many years of ignoring the feelings and attributing normal reasons to them had taken their toll on my skills. I knew it would be a very long time before I could state with certainty that I had sensed something predictive.

Neila stood and went to her cupboard. She pulled down a canister and scooped some of its contents onto a piece of waxed paper. She folded it carefully into the shape of a square envelope and handed it to me.

"Here," she said. "Try this in the evenings before you go to sleep. Just steep it in hot water for a few minutes—a teaspoon at a time will do. It might help you focus, or it might help make your dreams more illuminating."

I peered at the envelope and sniffed. Definitely chamomile . . . and something else.

"Thank you," I said. "I'll give it a try."

Neila nodded, but she had a distracted air. "Let me know if you get a better sense of what you are feeling. Do you want to stop by again before the weekend, or should we touch base after?"

I shrugged. "I'll come as soon as I have something to report."

"All right, dear," she said, and patted my hand. "Want to bring some cookies with you?"

I thought about my run that morning and shook my head. Mom would be in full-on comfort-food mode with Grace on the way anyway. I was sure cookies would be easily obtained for the foreseeable future.

3

Whenever my mom, my aunt, my sister, mean girls, or boyfriends had me upset, Diana was my go-to person. Wednesday afternoons were always slow at her shop, so I turned my car in the direction of downtown Crystal Haven.

My hometown admits with pride that it survives on the tourist trade. As I mentioned before, the only difference between Crystal Haven and every other lovely small town on the west coast of Michigan is the otherworldly attractions. Founded as a spiritualist community, it had morphed over the decades to include all manner of new age businesses. But I was surprised to see the streets so crowded this early in the season.

I drove past the Reading Room, where people met with psychics to learn about their past and future. The line snaked out the door. I had only seen that many visitors at the height of the summer season. We also boasted palm readers, tarot card readers, healers, and pet psychics. Visitors can purchase crystals, herbs, cards, crystal balls, books, and all the usual touristy stuff. They can also visit one of the best witch supply stores in Michigan.

Diana owns Moonward Magick and she runs it along with occasional help from an assortment of twenty-something assistants. I loved walking through the doors, and always felt as if I had stepped back in time. I knew the dark wood shelves held wands, cauldrons, and herbs, but I needed to wait for my eyes to adjust to the dark interior. I squinted through the haze of incense smoke before proceeding toward the counter where Diana frowned at a computer printout. Her springy orange hair fell over her forehead, and she pushed it back impatiently.

"Hey," I said.

Diana held up an index finger and muttered a string of numbers. She jotted something on her list and then looked up with a warm smile.

"Hey yourself," she said. "How's the training going?"

Based on the smirk that accompanied her question, I assumed she'd been talking to Seth or Alex. Alex, Diana, and I had been inseparable in high school, and since I had returned to Crystal Haven we were closer than ever. Seth must have regaled Alex with stories of my training troubles and Alex must have wasted no time in telling Diana.

I straightened my shoulders and ignored the tightness

in my legs. "Just fine. You know, no big deal." I waved my hand in what I hoped was a breezy gesture.

Her smile broadened. "You can always join our zombie team."

She and her boyfriend, Lucan, were heading up a small team of zombies for the Fun Run. Lucan was a private investigator and a runner through and through, but he had suffered a severe injury last fall while investigating a murder and was just starting to run again. Diana was a non-runner through and through, and it was only Lucan's injury that had kept her safe from my fate of running to appease a loved one.

"There's no way I'd be able to join your team even if I *could* desert the runners," I said. "Aunt Vi is taking this zombie apocalypse a little too seriously. I wish they hadn't started the costume contest. She's acting like the fate of the free world rests on this competition."

Diana laughed. "Well, if it's not a zombie tournament, it's a knitting spectacle. At least the parking meters are safe for a while."

After a recent knitting conference, Vi had become a militant yarn bomber. She had no cause or obvious statement to make, but that didn't stop her from covering benches, parking meters, and the occasional fire hydrant with colorful knitted items.

I grimaced and then sighed. Diana's smile fled and she narrowed her eyes at me.

"What is it?"

It didn't take much for Diana to realize something was bothering me. She reached forward to touch my hand but I pulled it away. I preferred to *tell* her about my sister and not convey my jumbled emotions through whatever weird connection we had.

"Grace is coming to town."

Her mouth dropped open slightly and her curls drooped. "When?"

"Later this afternoon." I broke eye contact because her dismay was feeding my own.

"But why? She hasn't been back in . . . what . . . ten years?"

We edged down the counter to let some customers examine the crystal balls and to get away from the chatter.

"Try fifteen." I said. "She never came back after she left for New York."

"Why now?"

I shrugged. "Apparently, she wants to support Seth in his charity run."

Diana pursed her lips. "I don't buy it."

I crossed my arms and leaned a hip against the counter. "Me neither. I just hope this isn't about wanting to bring Seth back to New York." I rubbed my forehead as a dull throb began. I held up my hand when I saw Diana's distress. "She hasn't said anything about that. When Seth went home at Christmas, he claimed they were just as busy and just as stressed. He said they seemed relieved he was so happy here."

"Grace has never been vindictive where the kids were concerned," Diana said. "She was always happy for them to come and visit your parents." Diana held up a finger and hurried around the counter to help a woman trying to squeeze a large frame into a small cloak.

"They've had several murders here, and now there's a zombie run!" I turned slightly to see who was speaking. A teen in goth makeup and all black clothing leaned conspiratorially toward her friend.

"Doesn't it creep you out?" the pink-haired girl with a nose ring whispered back.

The goth girl shook her head. "No, I think it makes this place even more interesting. It's not just psychics anymore, there might be ghosts."

"There are definitely witches." Her tongue stud clicked against her teeth causing a lisp. She looked around the store with wide eyes.

They moved off toward the book section and I couldn't hear them anymore. I sighed. I hoped Crystal Haven didn't really have a murder-town reputation. It had thrived on family centered, traditional readings and psychic offerings. The quaint and cozy surroundings encouraged visitors to stay.

I watched Diana with her customer and thought about my own family.

Things had been strained between my parents and my sister for years. While Mom and Vi delved fully into the psychic and fortune-telling aspect of our family's gifts, my mother had despaired that Grace had inherited nothing from her side of the family. Until Grace realized that the strings of numbers and letters that scrolled through her thoughts whenever she let down her guard actually correlated with the stock market readings. Once she recognized what she was doing, she begged my parents to let her invest their money. Unfortunately, during a fight with them over a boy, or car privileges, or some other teen drama, she ignored a warning feeling and lost everything in a devastating three-day downturn. It had cost my parents their house and most of their savings and now they lived with Aunt Vi. She had tried to repay them over the years, but they refused to allow it. Dad had forgiven her long ago, but Mom and Grace tiptoed around each other every time they were in the same room together.

Grace's son, Seth, was a different story. At fourteen, he had been unhappy in New York, unwilling to go to the boarding school his parents had chosen, and he had run away from home straight to my doorstep. Surprisingly, Grace and Paul had agreed to let him stay. I thought Grace suspected that Seth needed to be here.

Diana slid back behind the counter after sending the customer up front to the cash register.

I shook myself and tried to focus on the current concern. Other than the fifteen-year boycott of Crystal Haven, there was nothing unusual about parents wanting to visit their son, right?

I said as much to Diana, who tilted her head and reluctantly agreed. But in the silence between us, our worry grew.

I called Mac on my way home from Diana's to ask him to come to dinner at my mom's. He didn't understand all the intricacies of the situation, but knew that Grace coming to town was a big deal. He was wise enough not to actually say, "What's the big deal?"

Mac and I had dated seriously and broke up when

I was twenty-one and he was twenty-five. Eight years later, we had found ourselves back in Crystal Haven and learned that our breakup was due to a meddling friend and a colossal misunderstanding. We'd been back together for about six months when he moved in with me. I felt like I knew where we were heading, but instead of rushing forward, we were enjoying the adventure. Together with Seth, we made an unusual household, but it worked for us. This would be the first time Mac and Grace had seen each other in more than a decade and he had never met Paul.

"Okay, I've got this case to wrap up and then I'll head home," he said. "I'll meet you at your parents' if I'm running late."

I hung up and breathed out slowly. This would be fine. Mac would be there. Seth would be excited to see his family. It was all good.

4

I unclicked the dog leashes after a walk as Seth banged into the house. Tuffy ran to greet him, tail wagging so hard he almost fell over. The little dog stopped a few feet from Seth and his tail drooped slowly toward the ground.

Seth's hair stood on end and he had that barely contained energy that signified either excitement or anger. With a teenager, it was sometimes hard to know which one it was. But Seth had an easygoing personality and I had almost never seen him truly angry.

"Unbelievable!" he said. "Mr. Munson is going to ruin everything!" He threw his hands in the air and flopped onto the couch.

Anger it was.

Tuffy approached carefully and jumped up to sit

with Seth. He leaned against the boy and looked long-ingly into his face.

I saw Seth relax as he started to pet the little dog.

"What's wrong, dude?" Taking a cue from Tuffy, I moved slowly and, just to be safe, chose a chair a good distance from the couch.

"Mr. Munson is calling an emergency town meeting tonight," Seth said. He shifted his position so he could glower in my direction. "He's trying to get the zombie run canceled." Tuffy pushed his head under Seth's hand to keep the petting going.

"What? Why?" Thinking of how much time Seth had put into planning, I felt my own anger rising.

Seth sighed dramatically. "He says it takes away from the dignity of the Founder's Day weekend celebrations."

"Oh no."

"Oh yes. Alex went over there to try to talk some sense into him, but I think we're gonna have to go to the meet-ing tonight and plead our case."

The Munsons were my next-door neighbors and self-appointed town historians and rule enforcers. Harriett ran the Reading Room. Her husband, Lloyd, ran the Crystal Haven Historical Society. It was true that the big Founder's Day event was this weekend, but we had all assumed that the zombie run would only bring in more people and, since it was for a good cause, it wouldn't be a problem.

Traditionally, the Founder's Day celebration takes place on Saturday afternoon and evening. Lloyd arranges for a reenactment of the founder's story and then there's a bonfire in Greer's Woods, a parade, and an outdoor party until everyone gets tired. Seth's zombie run was scheduled for Friday night. I wasn't sure what Lloyd's issue was, but I was fairly certain Alex could talk him down.

"Alex will take care of it, Seth," I said. Baxter had wandered over to me and leaned against my leg to indicate he could use some attention as well. I rubbed his ears and tried to figure out how we would juggle Grace's return *and* a town meeting. There was no way to cancel the meeting once it had been called, but maybe we could calm the waters a bit beforehand.

Seth pulled Tuffy onto his lap and glared out the window. "I hope so. The animals really need the money. The rescue league building needs a bunch of repairs and if they're going to remain a no-kill shelter, they need cash to take care of all the animals."

I saw Seth sit a little taller and crane his neck to look out the window. I looked out as well. Alex strode across the grass between the Munsons' yard and my own. He knocked twice on the front door and came inside. Tuffy braced himself against Seth's chest and began barking, but stopped when he realized who it was. Baxter ambled over to Alex and pushed his forehead into Alex's hip. Alex was in and out of the house all the time. He'd moved to Crystal Haven in middle school and he, Diana, and I had immediately bonded. He owned Everyday Grill, the best restaurant in town, and that's not just his best friend talking. He came out to his family after high school and moved to Chicago, where he met his partner, Josh. They both moved back a few years before I did, and Josh opened The Daily

Grind. Josh's scones were almost as much of a tourist attraction as the psychics.

When Seth moved in with me last fall, Alex began teaching him how to cook. They had never gotten past pancakes, but they'd struck up a friendship, and the two of them had cooked up this fund-raiser for the animal shelter.

"Hey, buddy." Alex knelt down to look Baxter in the eye. His dark curly hair fell onto his forehead as he bent toward the dog—a sure sign he'd been running his fingers through it in frustration. The big dog rested his chin on Alex's shoulder. Alex didn't seem to notice the drool. I could tell he was trying to calm down before telling us about his visit with Lloyd. He'd had his own run-ins with Lloyd. As head of the Historical Society, Lloyd had the final say on construction permits, a strange bylaw that had never been voted out. It seemed all the business owners in town had to deal with Lloyd for any changes to their storefronts.

"What happened next door?" I asked.

Alex stood, shaking his head. "Those two are infuriating," he said. "They nodded and smiled at everything I said and then told me we'd have to put it to a vote."

"That's great, then," Seth said. "Practically the whole town is involved in the run, they'll all vote for it."

Alex nodded. "I think you're right, but Lloyd will play up the whole dignified angle. He thinks the zombies will lend a kitschy, casual feel to the weekend. Plus he thinks it might attract the 'wrong element,' whatever that is."

I wondered if Lloyd was right based on what I had seen earlier today in town. There were certainly more people wandering the streets than I would have expected. And the idea that they were coming because of the recent murders worried me. I didn't want Crystal Haven to become known for its tragedies.

Alex walked to the couch and flung himself onto it next to Seth. The two of them sighed.

I shifted into jollying mode. "It's going to be fine," I said. "I'll tell Vi to get her cronies together and start a phone tree—we'll call around and be sure we have a good turnout of supporters. What time is the meeting?"

"Eight," Alex said.

"Don't forget, Nana Rose wants us to come to dinner tonight," I said to Seth. "You're invited as well, Alex."

"I can't tonight. I have to get ready for the meeting," Seth whined.

"Clyde, we really need to prepare," Alex said. "I can feed him something at the restaurant and we can meet you at eight."

I tilted my head toward the kitchen and raised an eyebrow at Alex.

He sighed, pushed himself off the couch, and followed me out of the living room.

"Don't let her bully you!" Seth shouted after us.

Alex's reaction to the news of Grace's arrival was much the same as Diana's. He knew her less well than Diana, having moved to Crystal Haven just a year or so before Grace left. I felt guilty that his impressions of my sister were from unflattering stories of our childhood.

She was nine years older than me, and I'm sure my teen-aged view of her had been a heady mixture of hero worship and abandonment anger.

"Okay, we're going to your grandmother's for dinner," Alex said to Seth when we reentered the living room.

Seth nodded. "You always let her win," he grumbled.

"It'll be fine," Alex said. "I'll see you guys over there at six."

Alex let himself out and Seth crossed his arms and frowned at me.

I frowned back and dialed Vi's cell phone. After I had explained the problem to her, I turned the phone over to Seth and the two of them plotted their strategy and made lists of who to call to be sure the vote went in their favor. I used the landline to call Diana and got her working as well. I wouldn't have put it past Lloyd to selectively inform people of his emergency meeting— we needed to be sure *everyone* knew, and not just his anti-zombie crew.

At five thirty, we finished all the phone calls just as I heard Mac's truck pull into the driveway.

The wooden porch echoed his footsteps and the dogs ran to the door, Tuffy barking like a lunatic and Baxter already wiggling his entire body. Mac could never enter the house without a full-on welcome from the dogs. He'd been living here for more than two months but they still acted like he was visiting royalty.

Seth hopped up from the couch and gave Mac a quick wave in passing as he went upstairs to change before dinner.

"Hi, Seth," Mac said over the exuberance of the dogs.

I waded into the melee, sent Tuffy upstairs with Seth, and told Baxter to go lie down. Both dogs sighed heavily but did what they were told.

I stepped forward to greet Mac in my own way and I tried to enjoy the moment before the stress of the rest of the evening began.

"How was your day?" I asked. I kept my arms around his waist, looked up into his blue eyes, and noted the lines of fatigue and worry at the corners.

"We wrapped up the case, finally," he said. "So I'm caseless for now." He ran a hand over short blond hair and smiled, transforming the creases of concern into happy crinkles. "I'll be all ready for the zombie run as long as nothing comes in for the next couple of days."

"About that," I said. I released him and crossed my arms. "Lloyd Munson has called an emergency town meeting for tonight."

"But I thought we had to go to your mom's place for dinner," he said. He lowered his voice and glanced up the stairs. "Is Grace in town yet?"

I shook my head. "I don't think so. Vi said she'd text me if they arrived early. They want us there at six and think Grace will get there around six fifteen."

"When is Lloyd's meeting?" Mac looked at his watch.

"Eight, at the Reading Room."

"What's so urgent that he needs to call a meeting now? I'm not getting involved in the reenactment no matter what he says." Mac held up his hands like I was the one trying to rope him into wearing 1850s clothing and pretending to be an early townsperson.

"He's protesting the zombie run. He thinks it's unseemly."

Mac and I stepped into the living room and sat on the couch after displacing Baxter.

"He already had his chance. He was voted down." Baxter laid his head on Mac's knee and gazed up at him.

"I think he hopes the supporters will conveniently not attend and the second vote will go through."

Mac stood up abruptly, dislodging Baxter and earning an irritated sniff from the dog. "I'll talk to him. This is ridiculous."

I grabbed his hand and pulled him to sit next to me. "It's fine. We've got it covered. All of the zombie run participants will be there and he'll be voted down again. The whole thing will take ten minutes, and then Lloyd will have to accept it as a done deal."

Mac glanced at his watch again. "I'd better change if we need to be there at six."

Ten minutes later, Mac, Seth, and I clipped leashes on the dogs and set out for the two-block walk to my mom's. We walked up the long gravel drive, our shoes crunching the small stones. Seth scuffed his feet and kicked up rocks and dust.

Surrounded by tall aspens that lent a gloom to the yard even on a sunny day, my parent's house looked haunted, an impression my mother did nothing to alleviate. A gray Victorian, with steeply pitched eaves, the spires and vertical white accents made it seem taller than it's three stories. Its wraparound porch brought to mind simpler times, but I could never shake the feeling of someone watching from the shadows.

Vi greeted us at the door and ushered us quickly into the living room.

"Your mother is having a freak-out in the kitchen. Something about the gravy not thickening," she said. She lowered her voice, "She wants everything to be perfect. As if a pot roast will fix everything between her and Grace. I'd stay in here if I were you." She gestured toward the living room, an abomination of excess Victorian décor.

We sat stiffly on the Victorian-era couches that contained too many fringed pillows to accommodate actual people. The large clock on the mantel ticked each second in its melancholy fashion as Mac, Seth, and I tried not to knock over any of Mom's knickknacks.

Dad wandered in looking befuddled, but brightened when he saw us. "Where's your mother?" he asked. He was normally a little taller than me, at five foot ten. And his shock of white hair added a couple of inches, but tonight he was hunched and worried looking. He wore khakis and a plaid button-down shirt with a wool vest. The vest marked it as dressing up and I could only assume it was for Grace's arrival.

"Vi says Mom's having a crisis in the kitchen," I told him.

"Oh, we'd better stay out of there," he said. "Is Vi with her?"

"I think so," I said. "She told us to wait here and hurried off into the other room."

Dad sat on the edge of one of the armchairs. We settled into an uncomfortable silence. A crash from the kitchen made us all jump. The doorbell rang.

Dad hopped up and hurried to the door.

"Oh, hello, Alex," Dad said. "They're all in here."

Dad led Alex into the room and stepped back out again. Alex said hello to Mac and me.

"I think we'll be fine tonight, Seth," Alex said. "We've got plenty of zombie runners coming. Don't worry,"

The doorbell rang again.

"Jeez, how many people are coming to dinner tonight?" Seth asked.

Dad's voice floated in from the dining room. "Can you get that, Seth?"

Seth sighed dramatically.

Mac and I exchanged a look and followed Seth into the front hall.

Seth swung the door open and his face froze in a half smile.

"Mom? Dad? Soph?"

I caught a glimpse of Grace's long honey blonde hair as she stepped forward to hug Seth.

"I missed you so much, sweetheart," she said.

Seth looked embarrassed. He glanced at me and then back to his mom. "I missed you, too."

Within seconds the front hall was filled with excited squeals of welcome as Mom and Vi hurried out from the kitchen. Paul and Sophie took turns hugging Seth and between all the handshaking and hugging, the dogs wove in and out of the crowd in their own brand of greeting.

"It's good to see you, Clyde," Grace said as she hugged me tightly. I was enveloped in a cloud of Chanel No. 5. I had to take a step back to steady myself when she released me. Paul shook Mac's hand as Grace introduced them. And Alex got dragged into the greetings when Grace noticed him standing in the doorway.

Paul had never been to Crystal Haven, and Vi insisted on a tour of the house. She sent Seth and Mac upstairs with the bags while she dragged Paul down the hall to her apartment.

My feeling of unease had only intensified now that Grace was here. Her presence in the house where I had grown up had me on edge. Knowing that she had shunned Crystal Haven made me feel protective of it. So far, she was acting unusually bright and happy. It was a testament to my worry that I was miffed she was being so pleasant. I stood off to the side with Alex and watched as my mother and aunt fawned over Sophie and quizzed Grace on the flight.

"It was just fine, Mom," Grace said. "No troubles."

Seth and Mac returned just as Vi reentered with Paul.

"Well, dinner is ready," Mom said. "Let's eat and we can hear all about the trip."

We tromped into the dining room, with the dogs close on our heels.

Chairs shifted as the new guests shuffled into the usual seating arrangement. Sophie displaced Dad, who usually sat next to Seth. She hadn't taken her eyes off him since she'd arrived. At seven years old, she idolized her older brother. I wondered if that was how I used to look at Grace—naked hero worship and adoration on display.

"Just a little for me, Mom," Grace said. "I'm cutting back on meat."

Mom stopped, her spoon midway between the platter and Grace's plate. A large drip of gravy fell on the tablecloth. I could have kicked Grace. Didn't she recognize Mom's peace offering? Mom took a rejection of her food very personally. Fortunately Seth didn't notice the tension.

"I can't believe you guys are here," Seth said with a wide grin. He shoved his plate toward Mom and gestured that she should fill it up. "What about work?"

Paul took a breath to speak but Grace put her hand over his. "Don't worry about us, Seth. We've got the whole weekend to enjoy your zombie extravaganza."

"I want to be on your team, Seth," Sophie said.

"You've always been a fast runner," Seth said. "Do you think you can outrun Aunt Vi and her zombies?"

"Sure I can!" Sophie bounced in her seat and held up three fingers. "I'm the third-fastest girl in my class."

"You'll certainly give Vi a run for her money," Dad said.

"What money, Papa?" Sophie said. She wrinkled her brow at Dad.

"It's just an expression, sweetheart," Grace said. "It just means you'll be good competition."

"It sounds like Seth will get Grace and Sophie for his team—do you need any more zombies?" Paul asked Vi.

"Of course I do!" Vi said. "I knew this would work out just great. You can be our pirate zombie. Rupert Worthington was going to do it and then decided he wanted to be a doctor zombie instead. It's really no good without a pirate."

"Aargh! I'd be happy to be a pirate," Paul said.

Sophie giggled.

Detailed discussions of the costumes and makeup techniques ensued. The rest of us tried to focus on our food while Vi described how to make realistic looking blood and melting flesh. It wasn't easy.

"I'm really going to enjoy getting to know Crystal Haven this weekend," Paul said when Vi finally fell silent.

Mom beamed at him and offered more pot roast. Paul held up his hand and patted his slim stomach. Mom's smile wilted, but Seth saved the moment by shoving his plate forward. I wondered if he was more aware of the undercurrents than I thought.

"Can I have extra gravy, Nana Rose?" Seth said as she piled more meat and potatoes on his plate. "How do you make it so smooth?"

The corner of Mom's mouth twitched upward. Vi kept her eyes glued to her plate, but I could tell she was smiling.

"What's so funny, Vi?" Grace said.

"Nothing," Vi said. "Sometimes I think funny things."

"I do that, too," Sophie said. She nodded seriously at Vi.

"Sophie has a great sense of humor." Grace smiled at her daughter. "Why don't you tell Nana Rose that knock-knock joke?"

Sophie launched into a string of knock-knock jokes and I tuned in to the conversation between Dad and Paul.

"My new scanner can get signals from Grand Rapids and sometimes I even pick up stuff from the Indiana border," Dad said.

"So you listen to the police reports? As a hobby?" Paul failed to cover his surprise.

Dad lowered his voice. "Not always. Sometimes I just go and think my own thoughts without anyone trying to predict my next move."

Mac chuckled at this and Paul smiled.

"I'm very lucky Grace can only tap into the stock market," Paul said. "At least my thoughts are safe."

"As far as you know," Grace said. She grinned at Paul.

Mom's eyebrows rose and she looked at Grace.

"No, Mom," Grace sighed. "I haven't developed any more psychic ability."

"Oh. Well, you don't need it," Mom said. "You seem to be doing just fine."

Grace looked down and moved her food around her plate.

Sophie broke the uncomfortable silence. "Can you really read minds, Nana Rose?"

Mom was in midsip and coughed on her water. "Read minds?" She glanced at Grace. "No, hon. I can read tarot cards, but I can't tell what you're thinking. Except, of course, after dinner when I know you're thinking about either ice cream or cookies."

Sophie grinned. "I might be thinking about *both*!"

"Just as I predicted," Mom said.

Everyone laughed except Seth, who was so focused on his food a tornado wouldn't have distracted him.

Paul sat back in his chair and watched Seth devour a second helping of everything.

"How's school going, Seth?" Paul asked.

Seth looked up and mumbled, "Fine." He continued to work his way through his food.

I knew better than to try to get any information out of Seth when he was eating, but Paul continued.

"Are your classmates interesting?" Paul sipped his water and watched Seth over the rim of his glass.

I sensed a ripple of tension between Grace and Paul but didn't understand why.

"Yeah, they're great. I also have a friend, Logan, who volunteers at the animal shelter with me. He goes to a different school. He learned how to surf last summer and he says he'll teach me when the water warms up this year."

"Tell us about the animal shelter, Seth," Grace said.

Seth finished up his last bite and pushed his plate away. He shrugged, and looked down at his lap. "I like it there. The animals need people to feed them and play with them and I feel like I'm helping."

"It's not cutting into your schoolwork?" Paul asked. He leaned forward, resting his arms on the table.

Seth shook his head. "No, I'm doing fine."

Paul watched Seth carefully. "Have they started to teach you new stuff or are you still just reviewing?"

"It was only review for a little while, it's all new now."

Grace put her hand on Paul's wrist. He looked at her quickly and sat back in his chair.

"Well, I'm glad you're settling in, Seth," Paul said. He picked up his wineglass and finished it off in one long swallow. "Grace described it as the quaintest town in Michigan and so far I'd have to agree."

I caught a smirk pass between them before Grace covered her mouth with a napkin.

Grace turned toward Mac. "Clyde tells me you're all better after the shooting incident. Do you think you'll stay here in Crystal Haven now that you've recovered?"

The table fell silent. It was understood by everyone except Grace, apparently, that Mac did not like to talk about his injury. His leg hardly bothered him anymore, but I knew that no police officer leaves a shooting incident completely intact. The bullet is what had brought him back to Crystal Haven, but I knew *I* was the reason he stayed. Mac only ever discussed it with me and I didn't want him to think I had been telling my sister anything about his personal business.

He gently put down his fork and gave Grace a tight smile. "I have no plans to leave. I prefer quaint these days."

Grace had always been good at mentioning the one thing a person didn't want to talk about and then either ignoring or missing the signal to let it go. But even she picked up on Mac's reluctance to continue the conversation.

"Mac has been really busy recently," Vi said. "We even had to help him on a couple of his cases."

This conversation was rapidly spiraling out of control. Mac was extremely tolerant of my family's quirks, but he hated it when Vi tried to pretend she was his unofficial deputy.

"Let's have dessert!" Mom said. "Vi, why don't you help me in the kitchen?"

"But . . ." Vi glanced at my mother. "Okay." She pushed her chair away from the table and followed Mom to the kitchen.

Fortunately, Sophie had a *lot* of knock-knock jokes at her disposal and she kept us entertained and away from touchy subjects for the rest of the meal.

5

Vi rushed us out of the house at seven thirty. She said she wanted a good seat. In my experience, there wasn't a lot of competition for seats at one of these things, but maybe a special emergency meeting would be more popular. Plus there was the phone tree, and Vi was very persuasive.

Grace and Paul thought the whole idea of a town meeting "too charming" to pass up and they came along to support Seth. And, I suspected, to smile in a condescending way at the cute townspeople.

I had to pull myself together. So far, Grace had been nothing but pleasant. A less generous person would say she was being too pleasant. And I was trying to be generous. I still hadn't shaken the feeling that Grace was up to something, but I figured I should just wait and see what happened. Seth seemed happy that they had come and I didn't want to ruin that with my grumpy reservations.

We pulled up in front of the Reading Room and then had to park four blocks away. Mom had sent her spirit guides ahead to save us a spot, but they must have been on a break. When we arrived, the place was packed. I hadn't seen it this busy since the wake for a local Wiccan last fall. Usually the town meetings only drew the true political die-hards in town—basically, Lloyd, a couple of his friends, and whoever was there to argue with him.

It appeared the whole town had turned out for Lloyd's meeting. I introduced Paul to Diana, and Grace exclaimed at how much people would pay for her beautiful curls in the city. Diana smiled weakly, cast a quizzical look at me, and excused herself. Jillian Andrews, Mom's best friend, and her son Tom, who was a good friend and a new deputy in the Crystal Haven Police Department, approached to greet Grace, Paul, and Sophie. Sophie suffered through a lot of commentary on how big she was getting, as she hadn't been to Michigan in over a year.

We stood toward the back of the room, and endured the swarm of people acting as if Grace was a visiting celebrity. A man I vaguely recognized approached, and Grace smiled and pulled him into a warm hug. I was still trying to place him when Grace introduced him to Paul.

"This is my old friend Theo Lancaster," she said.

Paul nodded and shook hands with Theo as he had done with every other one of Grace's admirers.

I tilted my head and watched Theo. He looked nothing like the guy I remembered. He had been part of Grace's crowd after she graduated from high school. They would come to pick up Grace, or sit in our backyard and smoke cigarettes in that blatant way of early twenty-somethings who knew they were being ridiculous but dared anyone to stop them. He had been the only one of her friends who'd paid any attention to me at all. But *that* Theo had been skinny and shy, with long, dark hair that partly covered his eyes, and hardly ever spoke. This Theo seemed taller, confident, and even handsome. I saw him reach up and tug on his ear and it all came flooding back.

"Theo," I said. "It's good to see you."

He turned to me. His eyes widened. "Clyde?"

I nodded.

"It's great to see you," he said. "I'd heard you had moved to Ann Arbor."

"I've been back almost a year," I said. We grinned at each other and began asking the what-have-you-been-doing-with-your-life questions.

We had just begun almost shouting over the growing hubbub when I heard a voice I would never forget. It was smooth and warm, like hot chocolate on a cold day, and I suppressed a schoolgirl swoon.

"Well, if it isn't Amazing Grace," drawled the voice. "I never thought I'd see *you* standing in the Crystal Haven Reading Room ever again."

I turned to see Derek Vaughn. Grace blushed a slight pink, and Mom gasped. Theo's face went blank and he stepped back to let Derek take center stage. *That* was the Theo I remembered.

Time slowed as I watched Derek's smile spread. His warm brown hair was sprinkled with gray, and there were a few lines around his eyes. Mom stared, and Grace looked like she'd forgotten how to breathe. Derek pulled her into a hug that lasted several seconds longer than it should have. Grace pushed away from him and grabbed Paul's arm.

"It's nice to see you again, Derek," Grace said. "Meet *my husband*, Paul. And my children Seth and Sophie."

I caught Vi's eye and she raised her eyebrows and grinned like someone had just handed her tickets to a show. Derek and Grace had dated for three years before she left for New York. They had met in a business class at the local community college. Neither one of them passed, but, at least back then, Grace had said it was the best class she ever took because she met Derek. They'd only been engaged for a few weeks when Grace broke it off and fled to New York. Twenty-three seems young to get married, but I'm pretty sure Mom and Vi had already hired florists and caterers. He was no less handsome now than he had been then. I was fourteen at the time and thought he was the most elegant and charming man I had ever seen. I heard he'd left the area a year or so after Grace and, as far as I'd known, had not returned.

He turned to me. "Is this little Clyde?" His gaze

traveled slowly from my feet to my eyes and I felt my face growing hot. "Of course it is. No one else has eyes like that." He referred to my mismatched eyes—one dark brown and one light blue. I actually felt a shiver when he took my hand and kissed it. "You Fortune girls sure do age well. It must be the stunning genes from you two ladies." Just as he let go of my hand, I felt a warning. Not the kind that tells me to stay away, just a gentle nudge that all is not as it seems. It passed as quickly as it came and I wondered if I had imagined it.

Derek aimed his charm at my mother and aunt.

Mac stepped closer and put his arm over my shoulders. I noticed Paul take Grace's hand. Derek had that effect on people. The women swooned and the men closed ranks to protect the womenfolk.

"Oh, Derek, you're still such a flirt," Mom said and smiled at him.

"Where've you been all these years?" Vi asked. Vi jutted her chin at him and put her hands on her hips.

"Oh, here and there," he said. He kept his voice light and then turned to Grace. "We'll have to catch up while I'm in town."

Before I knew it, we were surrounded by Vaughns. Grace had pulled them like a magnet. Aaron, Derek's older brother walked over with his wife, Lila. I began to wonder why Theo, Derek, and the Vaughns were even at this meeting when I saw Aaron's son, Logan, and realized that, of course, he would be involved in the zombie run. Logan was shorter than Seth, closer to my five foot seven, with dark hair that he wore swooped up on top of his head like a melting soft-serve ice cream cone. This was the friend Seth had mentioned at dinner. Seth said it was nice to have a friend in another school because there was less drama, and the two boys bonded while cleaning out cages, playing with the dogs, and doing small repairs at the shelter.

The lights flickered on and off to signal that everyone should find a seat.

We surged toward the folding chairs that had been set out and Derek melted into the crowd. I saw him join his family at the other side of the room. His father, Richard, owned several high-end jewelry stores in Grand Rapids and along the coast of Michigan. I had heard that Aaron was taking over the business when Richard retired.

As I watched, Derek hooked a thumb over his shoulder in our direction. Richard shot a glance at us and seemed to linger on Mom and Vi. Mom wasn't paying attention, but Vi crossed her arms and pointedly turned her back to him.

The noise level grew as people jockeyed for seats. It quickly became clear that Harriet and Lloyd had not expected such a turnout and most of the crowd was left standing. Lloyd stood at the podium and pounded a gavel.

"All right! Everyone simmer down," Lloyd said. He slammed the mallet on the wooden stand and a shushing sound spread among the crowd.

Lloyd's eyebrows were up near his hairline and he cleared his throat.

"Well, I didn't expect so many of you today," he began. He scanned the crowd and I could tell he was tallying up the votes. He pulled on his bow tie. "It seems this is a much more sensitive topic than even *I* thought."

"Get on with it, Lloyd," Vi said.

He narrowed his eyes at Vi and then began. "As you all know, there is a charity run scheduled for Friday evening . . ."

The clapping and cheering swallowed his next words.

Lloyd held his hands up to shush the crowd. "Yes, well." Lloyd surveyed the gathering and placed the gavel carefully on the podium. "This is also the Founder's Day weekend."

There was more clapping, but it was polite and subdued.

Lloyd smiled at this and tugged on his vest. "As you all know, the Founder's Day celebration takes place on the last weekend in April every year to commemorate the founding of our wonderful little town of Crystal Haven."

The crowd was restless and whispers began. No one likes a midweek emergency meeting that only rehashes what everyone already knows.

"It is my feeling . . ." Lloyd raised his hands to silence the beginning rumblings from the back row. "It is my feeling as well as that of many others on the Founder's Day committee that a 'zombie fun run' is *not* the type of activity we want as part of our dignified celebrations of the birth of our town."

"What's dignified about standing around in the woods wearing moldy clothes and pretending to build houses?" Tom Andrews asked.

"Now, Tom," Lloyd said. "Your father was one of our best reenactors in his day."

"Oh yes, he was very good," Jillian said. She smiled at Tom. "The charity run won't interfere with the other events, Lloyd."

"That's not the point, Jillian." Harriet Munson stepped forward to stand next to Lloyd. "It detracts from the solemnity of the occasion."

"I think the flasks that get passed around the bonfire on Founder's Day are what detracts from the solemnity of the occasion," Charla Roberts, our chief of police, said. "I end up giving out more citations for drunk and disorderly on Founder's Day than on the Fourth of July!"

"You know that's not the point," Lloyd said and patted the air in front of him. He tugged on his bow tie again and his eyes darted around the room.

"So, what *is* your point, Lloyd?" Mac stood and crossed his arms. The crowd quieted. Seth gazed at him with admiration.

"My point is that the fun run should be moved to another, more appropriate weekend." Lloyd banged his gavel as if that was the end of the debate.

"We can't move it now," Seth said. He stood abruptly, scraping his chair. "The whole thing is set up, people are coming from all over just for the run, and the animals are desperate for this money—it will save the shelter!"

"Well, young man, you should have thought of that before you chose this weekend," Harriet said.

"I chose this weekend *because* it was the Founder's

Day weekend. I thought it would attract more donations for the shelter and it would jazz things up a bit."

Harriet puffed out her chest like an angry hen. "I don't think the celebrations need any 'jazzing' up. They are perfectly respectable just as they are."

"With falling turnout every year for the past ten years," said Alex. "We used to get people from all over Michigan and even from Chicago. It was the kickoff to the tourist season. Now no one comes until Memorial Day and Founder's Day costs more than it brings in."

Murmurs of agreement spread through the group, especially from the people who owned stores in Crystal Haven.

"That's just a small downturn," Lloyd said.

"Three percent every year, and ten percent for each of the past five years. If we keep going like this, there won't even be enough people attending to do the reenactment," Alex said.

Now the crowd was outright grumbling. Most of them hadn't been to the recent planning meetings where Alex had voiced these concerns.

"I think we should vote," Vi said. She was a master at reading a crowd and knew this was the time to strike.

"Vote! Vote!" said the crowd.

Lloyd raised his gavel and then lowered it slowly. He hung his head.

"All right!" Harriet said. She put her hands up. "We will proceed in a civilized fashion."

"All those in favor of moving the zombie run to another weekend, say aye," Lloyd said. He and Harriet said aye and then they gave the evil eye to a couple of their usual supporters who mumbled their assent.

"All those in favor of having the fun run this Friday night say aye," Vi said from her perch in the back row.

The response was loud and enthusiastic.

Lloyd tapped the gavel gently on the podium. "Motion passed," he mumbled.

Seth grinned and bumped his shoulder into mine.

6

Thursday morning I woke up later than usual with no kid to push out the door for school and no dogs to walk. I felt disoriented in my bright bedroom, listening to the quiet house.

Seth had somehow charmed his teachers into giving him Wednesday through Friday off *and* giving him extra credit for his community service project. He had decided to stay at my mom's with Sophie and his parents. He seemed thrilled to see his family again and I wondered for the fiftieth time if letting him move in with me had been the right choice. Tuffy stayed wherever Seth was and Baxter had made it clear he wasn't going to miss out on any of the fun or treats, so Mac and I had the house to ourselves for the first time since he moved in.

Mac's side of the bed was empty and cold. So he'd been awake for a while. I was about to get up when the door swung open and a rattling tray preceded Mac into the room. I smelled coffee and toast and eggs. Was there any question why I was crazy about this guy?

"Hey, are you awake?"

"Just. I thought you'd already gone in to work."

"No. No work for me today," Mac said. He placed the tray in front of me. "Remember I closed that case? I took the rest of the week off. As long as nothing big comes in, I'm all yours."

"Well, if you keep making breakfast in bed, I may not ever let you go back to work." I snagged a piece of toast and was glad that Vi was busy with her zombie team and had "closed" our business through the weekend.

"I have my own devious plans." He smiled his slow lopsided smile.

"Oh?" I dumped cream and sugar in the coffee and pretended I had no idea what he meant.

He watched me stir my coffee. "You'd better eat. You're going to need your strength."

An hour later, we heard my phone ringing from somewhere under the bed. I tossed on a T-shirt and rummaged for the phone.

"Don't answer it," Mac said. "It can't be good news."

"Your optimism is heartwarming," I said.

I found the phone and clicked it open to answer.

"Clyde. Hey, I texted you a bunch of times," Seth said. "Are you coming to help mark the route?"

My shoulders slumped. Of course. I had promised to

go through the woods with Seth and Alex and mark out the track for the run. We had already scoped out the best places to have the zombies waiting for the runners and we'd measured the distance, but we needed to place markers and directions to keep things moving on the day of the race. Mac was right—it wasn't good news, but at least it wasn't bad.

"Yes, sorry. I, uh, misplaced my phone so I didn't get your texts. I'll be there in twenty minutes."

"'Kay." Seth hung up.

"Told you," Mac said. "Want some help?"

"You want to tramp through the woods on your day off?" I tugged on my jeans and put my hair up in a ponytail.

"The weather's nice, and this way I can see where the zombies are going to be hiding. I don't want to scream like a little girl when they jump out at me." Mac was already pulling his shoes on.

"I kind of like the off-work Mac," I said and pushed him back onto the bed.

He pulled me with him and kissed me. Then he stood and held out his hand.

"We'd better get out of here before Seth comes looking for us," Mac said.

"He'd probably send Vi."

"All the more reason."

I took his hand and followed him out of the room.

Seth, Mac, and I arrived back at Mom's after two hours of tromping through the woods placing flags and arrow markers through the course. Alex went straight to his restaurant to help cover the lunchtime rush. We stomped our muddy shoes off on the front mat before ringing the bell. The door swung open and I yelped when I saw the creature standing before us.

It had pale gray skin, dark lips and eyes, and lots of blood. Blood was in her hair, dripping from her mouth, and oozing out of cuts on her face. Vi had combined all of the most horrible of her makeup tricks into one disgusting masterpiece.

"Oh, Vi, that is vile," I said. I looked away and pushed past her into the house.

"Good job, Aunt Vi," Seth said. He high-fived her and followed me.

A small and equally horrible zombie jumped out at us as we turned the corner into the dining room.

"Brains!" it said. "I need brains!"

It chased Seth around the table and he pretended to be terrified.

"All right, you zombies!" Mom said. She had entered the room with a tray of sandwiches. "It's time to eat. Sophie, can you go find your mom and dad?"

The small zombie grunted and limped out of the room, dragging one leg behind her.

Mom rolled her eyes and handed the sandwich tray to me.

"I'll be very glad when this is over," she muttered in my ear.

"Aren't you and Dad on the zombie team?" I asked.

Mom sighed. "Yes, we are. But I told Vi I would only be a zombie once. She can practice on the rest of the gang.

Your father is hiding in his den with the door closed."
She turned to Seth. "Can you go tell him lunch is ready?"

"Sure, Nana Rose," Seth said. "I'm sort of sad that
I'm on a running team." He turned to Vi, who was
trying to sit without tearing all of her shredded clothing. "Can you make me a zombie for Halloween?"

"No problem," Vi said. "I have tons of makeup now."

"Aren't you a little old for Halloween?" I said.

"Not if I can have a wicked zombie costume, I'm
not." Seth loped off toward Dad's man-cave.

Grace and Paul followed Sophie into the room.

"Oh, Vi," Grace said. "You look awful! I love it."

I think Vi smiled.

We sat and I managed to situate myself so I didn't
have to look at the undead while I ate. Dad was not so
lucky. He looked a bit green and pushed his food around
his plate.

"I was really surprised to see Derek Vaughn at the
meeting last night," Vi said. "I don't think he's been
back in town in years."

"I guess we're just lucky we chose this weekend to
visit ourselves," Paul said with a tight smile.

"Oh, don't you go getting jealous, Paul," Vi said.
"Like father, like son. Those Vaughn guys never had
a chance with Grace *or* Rose."

Dad put his head in his hands. Mom choked on her
water.

Sensing a shift in the mood of the table, Seth glanced
up from his food to look around for the source of the
disturbance. Mac, sitting next to me, was well-versed in

staying out of Fortune family drama. He kept his head down and focused on the remains of his sandwich.

"What are you talking about, Vi?" I asked.

Grace dabbed at her mouth with her napkin and glared at Vi.

"Let's not rehash the whole thing, Vi," Grace said.

"Rehash what whole thing?" Sophie said.

Vi looked at Mom and Grace, who wore matching censorious expressions.

"Oh, it's nothing, hon. Just ancient history." Vi flapped her hand and went back to her food.

"Does anyone want some brownies?" Mom asked brightly. "Vi, maybe you can help me in the kitchen." Her voice had become steely.

"Oh, okay." Vi pushed her chair back and stood.

"I'll help, too." Grace said, and tossed her napkin on the table.

This was too juicy to pass up. "I'll help," I said, and quickly followed them out of the room. I saw Dad and Mac relax as I turned the corner.

". . . bad enough that you constantly harass him about his career in dentistry, you don't need to bring up Richard," Mom said to Vi as I entered the kitchen. Grace stood with her arms crossed watching them both.

"What's going on?" I said.

"It's nothing," Mom said.

Grace tilted her head at Mom.

"Doesn't Clyde know?" Grace said.

"Know what?" I said. "What don't I know?" I crossed my arms to match Grace and looked from Mom to Vi.

Mom took the brownies off the stove and began vigorously cutting squares.

"You're turning it into a bigger deal than it is," Vi said. "I didn't mean to start anything. I forgot that not everyone knows about you and Richard."

"What about Mom and Richard?"

Mom pushed the brownie pan away and placed her fingers on the bridge of her nose, much the way I did when Vi tried to get me to do anything psychic.

Grace gently took the knife from Mom and finished placing the brownies on a plate.

"It's actually a very romantic story and your father is the hero," Vi said, "I don't know why she's being all secretive."

"I'm not being secretive, Vi," Mom took the brownie pan and began scrubbing it in the sink. "I just don't think we need to dredge up the past at a pleasant family meal."

Vi shrugged. It was still hard to look at her, but I forced myself.

"Okay, spill it," I said.

"Well, your father hates it when the subject comes up," Vi began.

"Which you obviously know, and yet you persist," Mom huffed.

Vi glanced at the door with her sunken, dark-circled eyes. It was so like my family that a zombie would reveal our dark secrets.

"Richard Vaughn and your mother dated all through high school and then got engaged right after graduation."

"What?" I said. "You were engaged?"

All three of them shushed me and I lowered my voice.

"Why am I just hearing about this now?" I whispered.

"For one thing, it's very far in the past—forty-five years to be exact. It doesn't matter anymore."

"I saw the way he looked at you," Vi said. "It's not the past for him,"

Mom blushed. "Vi, stop it. He's been married to Nora almost as long as Frank and I have been married. No one is harboring any unrequited love . . ."

"Okay," Vi said. "If you say so." Eyes rolled in her zombie face.

"I remember it was a pretty big deal when I started dating Derek," Grace said. "His mother threw a fit that he was dating one of your daughters."

"Both of you stop," Mom said. Mom held out her hands and then moved them to her hips. "The brownies are drying out. Let's go back in." Mom picked up the plate and sailed out of the room with her head high.

"I'll tell you the rest later," Vi said. She put a bony finger to her lips and then followed Mom out of the room.

"Is that all there is to it?" I asked Grace.

She nodded. "Mostly. I think there was an acrimonious breakup and there may have been some fisticuffs—Dad's word—between Dad and Richard the night before Mom and Dad's wedding, but it all finally simmered down. I knew about most of it from Derek. He'd heard the whole story from his parents when he told them we were dating."

I sighed. I felt like the nine year age difference between Grace and myself meant that I was always the last one to know anything. Not that this really mattered, I supposed. It was old news, not something to worry about now.

Grace peeked through the kitchen door to the dining room. She put her finger to her lips and tilted her head toward the back door. I was surprised she was going to tell me the story now. Back when we were growing up, she would hold this kind of information over my head for days before finally spilling.

She pulled the door open slowly, but Dad had fixed the creak years ago. We stepped out in the yard and Grace crossed her arms against the chill.

"I hoped I'd get a chance to talk to you alone," she said.

My shoulders tensed. She wasn't going to tell me the story of my mother's long-ago engagement. This was something else.

"Does Mac have to work tomorrow?" she asked. "I thought I heard him say he was off through the weekend."

I wasn't expecting this. "He's home tomorrow." I narrowed my eyes at her.

"Great," she said. She started pacing and muttering to herself about phone calls in the morning.

"Is there anything else?" I asked and let a snotty preteen tone slip into my question.

She stopped pacing and looked at me. "Yes, I just said." She gestured at the path she had been walking. "I'm going to call the lawyer tomorrow and try to set up a meeting at eleven. You can both make it, right?"

I noticed she hadn't asked if *I* was busy tomorrow before demanding this audience.

"Why?" I asked. I crossed my arms, to keep from putting my hands on my hips like Mom. "What's up, Grace?"

Grace glanced nervously toward the house and then scanned the backyard. I looked around as well and wondered what we were looking for.

"I'd rather not talk about it yet," she said. "Can't you just do this for me? Why does it always have to be so hard with you?"

I felt my eyebrows rise and I took a step back. I opened my mouth in shock and to say something I would likely regret.

"I'm sorry," she said. She shook her head as if to clear it and stepped forward to put a hand on my arm. "Please, Clyde. I feel like all I've done lately is ask for favors, but I really need both of you to come to Rupert Worthington's office tomorrow."

Her rapid shift from queenly proclamations to sincere-sounding request confused me enough that I agreed.

"Yeah, okay." I kept my arms crossed to let her know I was still miffed.

"Don't tell anyone but Mac," she said, and darted back in the house.

7

~≈≈~

Friday morning I stopped in at Diana's store again.

"How's it going with Grace?" Diana asked after we had settled in her office with tea.

"Not sure yet," I said. "Family secrets have been spilled and she wants me to meet her at the lawyer's, so only minor drama so far."

Diana leaned forward. "Family secrets? Tell me."

I waved my hand airily. "Something about my mother's checkered past and the broken hearts she trod upon as a youth."

"Your mom?" Diana tapped a finger to her lips. "I could see that. She's beautiful and just flighty enough to wreak havoc."

I tossed an eraser at her. "Don't trash-talk my mom."

Diana grinned. "Good thing she finally settled down."

"It does seem strange to think of Mom and Vi and Dad being involved in any sort of romantic entanglements," I said. "Grace says there was even a brawl or two between Dad and the jilted boyfriend."

"Frank Fortune brawling?" Diana shook her head. "Nope, that's where you lost me."

"Me, too. I can't picture my dad fighting with anyone. Except maybe Vi."

"What's with the lawyer?" Diana said.

I shrugged. "I assume it's something to do with Seth living here. Maybe they have to sign something for the school to let him stay enrolled?" I picked at a thread on my jeans. I was concerned. Grace refused to tell me what the meeting was about and I had no idea why she would need Mac there as well.

"They wouldn't have to come all the way here for that." She folded her hands on the desk and held my gaze until I looked away.

"No, you're right." I sipped my cooling tea. "Plus, she insisted that Mac come along." I blew out air. "She can be so annoying. I don't know why she has to make everything a big weird secret."

"Maybe she doesn't want your parents to know whatever it is?" She poured more tea into my cup and pushed the sugar bowl toward me.

"Maybe. I guess I'll find out soon enough."

We finished our tea and I told her about Vi's frantic search for the best zombie makeup.

"She told Lucan and me she'd give an award to the zombie team with the most kills." Diana's face puckered with distaste. "Sometimes I wonder about her mental health."

"Sometimes?"

Diana walked me back out to the front of her store. A young woman was there talking to Diana's assistant, Bethany. I felt Diana stiffen beside me. She sighed.

"Hello, again, Tatiana," Diana said.

Tatiana turned her sea-green eyes on us and brushed her silky blonde hair back behind her shoulder.

"Hi, Diana," she said. She managed to make it sound like a purr.

"This is my friend, Clyde Fortune." Diana gestured at me.

"Oh, it's lovely to meet you!" Tatiana said. "I've heard so much about you and I've only been here for a couple of days."

"Oh?" I looked to Diana for guidance, but she just shrugged.

"I opened last weekend and I've been fixing up my shop—it's right through there." She smiled and waved her hand at a doorway leading to a small store. Technically part of Diana's store; she had rented it out for years.

"But that's Tanya's shop," I said.

Tatiana nodded. "My cousin. She had an opportunity come up that she couldn't refuse, so she turned it over to me."

I had never gotten along that well with Tanya, so it

wasn't a loss to me, but I wondered what would make her leave so suddenly.

"Are you a palm reader, like your cousin?"

Tatiana shrugged. "I taught her everything she knows. Here, let me take at look at yours."

She grabbed my hand before I could step away and held it in a surprisingly strong grip.

"Let's see, a nice long life line. You spend a lot of time lost in your own thoughts . . . and oh, my."

"What?" I leaned forward in spite of myself.

"Gotcha!" Tatiana winked. "Just kidding. You stop by the shop and I'll take a proper look. See you soon, Diana."

"Bye, Tatiana."

The bell tinkled as she stepped through the connecting door.

"It's her favorite joke," Diana said. "She was in here the other day trolling for customers, getting them all worked up. I had to ask her to leave."

"Well, she's friendlier than Tanya," I said.

"I suppose. I get a weird vibe from her, though." Diana twirled a curl around her finger. "I can't quite figure her out."

"She was in here asking about athames," Bethany said.

Athames were ritual blades used in some Wiccan ceremonies. Diana didn't display them in her shop, but I knew she sold them to known customers.

"Really? What would she want with one of those?"

Bethany shrugged and went back to straightening the incense boxes.

*   *   *

The day was even warmer than Seth and Alex had hoped. I was glad we wouldn't be running that evening through dark, zombie-infested, cold, and wet woods. The dark and the zombies were enough. I met Mac at the gazebo in the park and we walked together to Rupert's office.

"Oh, good, you're all here," Rupert said as he greeted us in his front office. "Come on back. I sent Phyllis out on an errand, as Mr. and Mrs. Proffit stressed the sensitive nature of our meeting."

Mac met my raised-eyebrow look with one of his own and we followed Rupert into the inner office.

Grace and Paul turned as we entered, and Paul stood to shake Mac's hand.

"Sorry for the cloak-and-dagger routine," he said. "We didn't know any other way."

Mac and I sat in the two folding chairs Rupert must have pulled in from storage. The five of us barely fit in his small office, made even more cramped by the piles of paper and file folders stacked precariously around the room and on every flat surface.

"Let me just get the file here," Rupert said. He ran his fingers down the stack nearest him on the desk and chose one toward the bottom. He tugged, and the rest of the pile tottered. Grace grabbed the leaning pile and lifted it for Rupert.

Rupert seemed not to notice. It must be part of Phyllis's job description to keep the piles standing upright.

He flipped open the file. "I have all the paperwork ready to go here. Two versions, just as you asked," Rupert said. He nodded at Paul and Grace.

"Is anyone going to tell us what is going on?" Mac said.

"Yes, yes," Rupert said. He patted the air in front of him and turned to Grace. "Mrs. Proffit?"

"Paul and I wanted to ask the both of you if you would be willing to act as guardians for Seth and Sophie if anything should happen to us." She took Paul's hand.

"That's it?" I said. "You want me to be a guardian? I'm already doing that with Seth. Besides, nothing is going to happen to you."

"We'd like both of you to agree," Grace said, and looked at Mac.

"But we're not . . . married. We . . ." I trailed off. I hadn't expected this part.

"No, we know that. But, c'mon guys, you will be someday." Grace smiled at me. "You don't need to be psychic to see that."

I heard a roaring in my ears and my heart pounded. Leave it to Grace to ruin everything. Mac and I were in a great place. I had just gotten my mother to back off on her wedding hints, and now this.

"Grace, that is very presumptuous of you. Mac doesn't need to take on this kind of responsibility," I said, trying to control the edge that had crept into my voice.

"Clyde, it's fine." Mac put his hand on mine. He turned to Grace and Paul. "I assume you'll give us some time to discuss this?"

"Of course. But this is the part that we need to keep secret," Grace said. She glanced at the closed office door. "Paul and I are in trouble."

Mac leaned back in his chair. His cop face had appeared. "What kind of trouble?"

"Pretty scary trouble," Paul said. "We aren't asking this as a precaution against a freak accident. We're actually in danger."

"What? What are you talking about?" I said. "You guys are stockbrokers."

They exchanged a glance. Grace took a deep breath.

"We've gotten in over our heads in a situation that involves some very dangerous people." She held up her hands when I started to speak. "Just let me get this out. A couple of years ago, we took on a very big client and we made some investments for him that did really well. Then he referred a friend who wanted to invest a *lot* of money. We didn't realize that the friend was connected to the Milano family and in fact was using their money to make the investments. Just before the stock market tanked, I advised all my clients to restructure, but this client refused. He was making money hand over fist and he didn't want to stop. He thought we were just running scared like everyone else at the time."

Grace stood and walked to the bookcase. When she turned I saw tears glittering in her eyes. I felt my mouth twist in disbelief. Grace was the least emotional person I knew.

"I couldn't tell him how I knew for sure that he should pull out, and of course he lost a lot of money. The problem is, it wasn't his money. He was supposed to be managing the funds for the Milanos but he'd been skimming off the top and had to make up his losses." Grace swallowed hard and looked at Paul.

"They threatened us with . . . well, with an unpleasant death if we couldn't recoup the money." Paul leaned forward in his chair, hands clasped between his knees. "We did manage to get the money back but not without pretty blatantly using Grace's . . . talent. The SEC got wind of it and brought charges. Now, they can't prove insider trading because of course we didn't use any information we got from an insider and the feds don't really go in for the psychic investor story."

"Grace. I'm sorry," I said. "Seth told me he thought you guys were stressed at work but I had no idea."

Grace nodded at me and gave a weak smile.

"The problem is, the SEC has been crawling through our books and the FBI heard about our client. Now they want us to testify against them or face charges of our own."

Mac shook his head and put his arm over my shoulders.

"What are you going to do?"

"We aren't sure yet, but if anything happens to us, we want to be sure that the kids are safe. It's one of the reasons we were so willing to let Seth move here. We know it's a lot to ask, but we hope you'll agree to take Sophie as well. Paul has no family and it would be one less thing to worry about."

I looked at Mac. This was too much to ask.

"We have to talk about this, Grace."

"No," Mac said.

"No?" Grace asked.

"I mean, no we don't need to talk about it." He turned to me. "I know if it was just you, you'd take both kids without a second thought. You already took Seth in and I know how much you love having him around."

"But this is different, Mac," I said. "This isn't your responsibility."

"Yes, it is. If it involves you, it's my responsibility."

"You don't have to sign the papers right now," Paul said. "And it may not ever come to anything. But if we could have an answer before the end of the weekend, that would put our minds at ease."

"Mr. and Mrs. Proffit have already signed." Rupert pointed to the signatures. "Whenever you're ready, you can both sign and you will become legal guardians of Seth and Sophie upon their parents' demise."

We left Rupert's office together. Paul and Grace walked back toward Mom's house and Mac and I turned toward The Daily Grind. We were in desperate need of some coffee and one of Josh's scones.

I turned to say something to Mac and noticed a couple of guys wearing dark suits across the street looking at a map. Crystal Haven only has one main street—a map is hardly necessary. I got a weird tingling on the back of my neck as I watched. One was tall with dark hair, cut short and close, giving his head a rounded appearance. His jacket tugged across his shoulders as he held out the piece of paper. The second one was shorter and wore a blond flattop style. He pushed the map down so he could look over the top. They both seemed to be watching Grace and Paul rather than studying anything on the map. Grace tugged on Paul's hand when they got to the corner and the two of them turned toward the marina. The two suits glanced up and down the sidewalk and then quickly folded the map and walked in the same direction Grace and Paul had gone.

All of this happened in less than twenty seconds.

Mac was talking about what kind of scone he was going to have and didn't notice I had stopped walking until he was already several strides ahead of me.

"Clyde?" He turned and walked back to where I stood. "What's up?"

"Those guys there, in the suits," I said, and pointed discreetly up the street. Not that they were paying any attention to us.

"Yeah, I see them."

"I think they're following Grace and Paul."

"What? Why?"

Just as he said that, the two men turned into Alex's restaurant.

"Oh," I said. "Maybe not."

Mac smiled. "Grace just has you spooked with her guardian paperwork and stories of mob connections."

He slung an arm over my shoulder and turned me in the direction of coffee and scones.

8

That evening Mac and I stood shoulder to shoulder in the deepening gloom. The weather had turned on us, April being the most fickle month. The cooler temperatures and slight mist that hung in the spaces between the trees forced me to try to picture the faces of the puppies and kittens at the shelter. Knowing the woods were teeming with crazed zombies egged on by Vi's contest meant I required all of the maturity I could muster to stay at the starting line.

Seth and Alex must have sensed my misgivings because I felt them closing ranks behind me. Each runner had three "lives," or flags, attached to his or her waistband. A zombie could only take one flag from each runner, but now thanks to Vi, the zombies were excessively interested in collecting the scraps of fabric. What had started as a somewhat whimsical way to structure a 5K charity run had turned into a survival drill.

Alex pulled us into a huddle for his pep talk.

"Okay, team," he began. "If we're going to survive the zombie apocalypse, we're going to have to trust each other."

I glanced around the circle. Mac, Grace, Alex, Seth, Josh, and Tom Andrews were all part of team Tuffy. Sophie had deserted us for Vi's zombie team after she had tried on the makeup. There were five other teams running and the one with the most members still alive at the end of the run would double their money earned. A large dog food manufacturer had promised to match the donations for the winning team.

"Here are the rules: One, no man gets left behind—especially if they still have flags left. Two, keep the ones with the fewest lives toward the center of the pack. Three, no drama—I know some of the zombies look scary, but we don't need to panic, they're just people."

"Plus most of them chose a zombie team because they aren't very good runners," Seth added.

"Four, no whining." Alex looked at me when he said this and I have to say, I took umbrage at that. Tom was just as likely to whine as I was.

We held our hands in the center of the circle for a team chant.

"This is for the orphaned animals," Seth said. "Go Team Tuffy!"

The other teams lined up. We were in the second

round. Two teams would be released every five minutes—
to give the zombies a chance to attack as many people as
possible, I assumed.

Mayor Winchester shot the starting pistol and the
first two teams raced ahead. There were no rules as to
how to treat the other teams and I was concerned that
there would be some intra-team fighting if things got
tricky in the woods.

We lined up next to our partner team. They were
from the local medical clinic—three nurses, two doctors, a respiratory therapist, and two receptionists.
None of them looked very compassionate. They looked
like they would throw us to the hordes the first chance
they got.

Two minutes before it was our turn to go, we heard
shrieks from the woods. The first set of zombies must
have appeared.

"Okay, this is good info," Alex muttered to us. "Three
minutes in and we'll hit the first wave. Be ready."

I was edging toward the center of the pack when the
gun went off. Grace pushed past me and I found myself
on the outside edge of the crowd. I hated running so
much, and now I was heading into the dark, damp,
zombie-infested woods. How did I let myself get talked
into these things? I hoped I could keep up with my gang.
I didn't want to be the reason we all got massacred.

Just as I hit my stride and passed that point where
every muscle was arguing against this fiasco, the first
set of zombies approached. They technically weren't
allowed to run, but they sure were moving fast. We

moved as a group to the left to avoid the clutching hands, but, just as quickly, the next group appeared. The medical team was on the right side and they hit the zombies head-on. The nurses and one of the doctors started screaming until the receptionist took over and shouted orders. We veered to the right and one of the zombies snagged Seth's flag.

"I'm hit!" he said and we all adjusted to let him move to the center.

"Let's move, team!" Alex shouted.

I felt the group pick up speed and I tried to keep up with them. Mac grabbed my hand and pulled me along. Grace tripped over a branch and went down. Tom stopped to help her up and a zombie got one of his flags. The medical team was still shouting and Alex steered us over to them.

"Stay with us, the next safe zone is just up ahead," he said to the other group.

That energized them and we all sprinted to the white flag. We'd have about three hundred meters of safety before we'd enter another zombie zone. Runners were not allowed to loiter in safe zones and could lose a flag if caught. We slogged through the muddy trail, a little less enthusiastically than before.

I noticed the medical team hung back as we approached the end of the safe zone. Cowards. They obviously wanted us to be the guinea pigs for the next area. My team slowed as we crossed the line and we took up our positions to scan the woods for zombies. Josh was assigned the role of running backward as much as possible to be sure we weren't attacked from behind. Even though we had marked the areas, the zombies had been given access to their zone to choose their strategy and hiding place.

I spotted a Girl Scout zombie among the trees and I let out a sigh of relief.

"Two o'clock, in the trees," I said.

The Girl Scout was Sophie's costume. Surely Vi's team would go a little easy on us. I saw the pirate just behind Sophie—that was Paul—and then I saw Vi's horrible, decaying bride of Frankenstein getup.

Then many things happened at once.

Josh yelled, "Mayday!" This was the signal that we were being attacked from behind.

Alex shouted, "Nine o'clock!"

The Girl Scout ran straight at me and grabbed a flag, while Grace grappled with the pirate.

The medical team came upon the scene and veered toward the left, straight into the second zombie team that Alex had seen.

There were zombie faces and hands everywhere and we broke ranks to run as fast as we could for the next safe zone. Even though I knew who all the zombies were, the fear and adrenaline hit my system and I took off running. I heard someone stumble behind me and against all my instincts I turned to help Seth disentangle himself from a pile of loose branches that had been thrown across the path. Mac and Alex ran toward us with Grace in between them—she had lost another flag and only had one left. We had vowed not to lose a member, but we had two more zombie zones to get through before the finish. Josh took up the rear and seemed to be limping, but the zombies had stopped chasing us and had focused on the medical team.

We slowed down in the next safe zone, just enough to assess the damage to the team.

Grace was the only one down to just one flag. We moved her toward the center of the pack. Alex and Mac still had all their flags. Alex took the front position and Mac took the back.

The scoring system was complicated. A team with all members still "alive" at the end of the run got a big bonus point boost. However, each individual with all three flags also earned bonus points. The rules allowed for a one-time transfer of a flag from a member with three flags to a member with one. A team could not resurrect a member after that person had lost all their flags. Alex and Seth had run the numbers obsessively and knew the ramifications of each choice. Grace needed another flag, and either Alex or Mac would be able to give her one.

Seth and Alex discussed strategy in hushed, urgent tones. Mac jogged next to them and volunteered one of his flags.

"We still have to get through Diana and Lucan's team as well as the team from Everyday Grill," Alex said. "I don't know if my staff will go after me or go easy on me, and the same goes for Diana and Lucan. They might choose Mac instead to avoid any worry about repercussions later. But Mac and Tom are police, so they might avoid chasing them as well."

Seth nodded. "I think it's an even split—we just have to choose and hope for the best."

Mac nodded. "Seth's right. We can't predict what they'll do and it all comes down to opportunity anyway."

"Okay, Mac, you give Grace one of your flags and we'll hope that my employees will go easy on me. I can't say I have the same hopes for Diana."

Mac pulled a flag out and handed it to Grace, who tucked it into her waistband.

We crossed over into the next zombie zone and were greeted immediately by Diana's team. This gang was playing a little more according to the no-running-zombies rule and though they limped and hobbled quickly, we escaped with only the loss of one of Tom's flags. The zombies then turned their attention to the clinic team—this time hanging back had been the wrong choice. The zombies were waiting for them and didn't have to move very fast to be able to snag a couple of flags, or at least that's what I assumed based on the zombie cheering I heard rising behind me.

We now had about a mile of woods to get through, including crossing the river, before we would meet any more zombies. The last two zones had only been assigned one team of zombies each.

I was tired and felt clammy from sweat and the cool damp air. Seth ran next to me muttering to himself. I thought he said, "Puppies and kittens, puppies and kittens." But I couldn't be sure.

I saw the flag that signaled the next zombie zone. I also spotted one of the teams that had been released ahead of us. They must have loitered somewhere for us to catch up to them.

Alex ran ahead of us and signaled that we should try to skirt around to the right—the zombies were busy with the other team and maybe we could get through without too much trouble.

The minute we crossed the line of flags the zombies deserted the other team and headed in our direction.

"Alex!" they said.

"Oh, no," Seth said. He turned and shouted to the rest of the team. "Put Alex on the inside!"

Chaos ensued. The zombies swarmed us and I lost another flag. Mac was down to one flag and we put him at the center. Since Alex still had all three flags we had to move him to the outside, which got the zombies very excited. Josh hip-checked one zombie to get her to back off her relentless pursuit of Alex and the rest of us sped up to get away from them. Seth and Tom both lost a flag and Alex lost two before it was over, but we burst into the safe zone with every team member still alive. Barely.

Covered in mud, Josh, Mac, and Tom all limping, we staggered over the finish line. The end of the race had been set up in Message Circle. It was a clever marketing ploy on the part of the mayor, who insisted that if there were going to be spectators, they might as well wait in Message Circle. It was a free-sample kind of place where psychics shared messages with the audience. I don't think anyone missed the fact that a short message often led to a longer paying session.

Seth jumped up and down with renewed energy at finishing with an intact team. I lurched toward the water table and felt more like a zombie than a runner. Back slapping and general hilarity ensued as the team realized we were safe and we had finished.

We sat on the ground and on the benches arranged in an arc around Message Circle. Alex and Seth returned from the judge's table to report that our team was in the lead.

9

~ୱେଡ଼ିବ~

The evening air cooled around us as we lounged and ate cookies in Message Circle while the woods grew dark. Seth entertained us with impressions of Grace and Alex running from zombies and we cheered the remaining teams as they arrived. The fresh tang of old leaves and new growth faded as the wood smoke from the bonfire filled the air.

Finally, the last team straggled over the finish line and the mayor blew his air horn to signal the zombies to come and join the runners for the costume contest. We heard them crunching through the forest as they approached Message Circle. Some of them stayed in character and limped or dragged their legs. Others walked normally and were clearly looking forward to becoming human again.

"Aunt Vi did a better job on the makeup than that team," Seth whispered to me as the Everyday Grill gang lurched past our bench.

"This group looks good," I said.

"I think that's Logan's team," Seth said.

I had turned in my seat to see if I recognized any of the Vaughn Jewelry team when Grace came up to us with a wild look in her eye.

"Have you seen Sophie and Paul?"

Seth and I shook our heads.

"They're probably with Vi, wherever she is," Seth said. He spun around on the bench and looked toward the food table.

Grace shook her head. "I just talked to her and she hasn't seen them since they were in the woods. *She* asked *me* where they were."

I scanned the crowd. "They must be here somewhere," I said. I spotted Mac talking to Alex and walked over to where they stood.

"Have you guys seen Sophie or Paul?"

They both shook their heads and started to look around the clearing just as I had done.

Grace came up behind me.

"Where could they be?" She shivered and hugged her arms across her chest.

"Did you try calling Paul?" Mac asked.

Grace nodded. "It's just going to voice mail. I don't think I get a very good signal out here in the middle of nowhere."

"They can't have gone far, but they might have gotten

lost in the woods," I said. It was dark outside Message Circle's bonfire and torches, and someone unfamiliar with the woods could easily lose his or her way.

"I'll go get some flashlights from the judge's table." Alex strode to the other side of the circle.

Seth rounded up Mom, Dad, and Vi and we prepared to head back into the woods.

"Let's split up into pairs," Mac said. "Clyde, you and Grace head east. Rose and Frank, south. Seth, Alex, and I can head west. I doubt they passed through Message Circle, so let's meet back by the bonfire in fifteen minutes."

"What about me?" Vi said.

"It's most likely they'll arrive here before anyone gets back," I said. "Wait here and keep an eye out for them."

I knew she didn't want to be late for the costume contest, so she happily accepted this assignment.

Diana and Lucan rushed up to us looking worried. "What's the matter?" Diana asked.

"Paul and Sophie are missing—we're going back into the woods to look for them," I said.

"I have my car at this parking lot—Diana and I can drive around to the south lot where the race started and see if they ended up there." Lucan took Diana's hand and they moved back through Message Circle.

We made plenty of noise as we spread out through the woods. I tried to keep Grace calm, but walking through dark woods with a weak flashlight beam, shouting your child's name, isn't something that a mother can do calmly.

After we got about five minutes from Message Circle, we couldn't hear much from the gathering of zombies and runners.

"You go that way, and I'll head this way toward the bridge," Grace said. "We can cover more ground. Let's just make sure we can still hear each other."

I nodded and took the path toward the right. I shone my light along the dirt track and into the undergrowth. I had no idea why they would have ended up in this section of the woods; it was too far from where the run had been and too far from Message Circle. But neither one of them knew these woods the way the rest of us did. Maybe they got separated from the crowd and then got lost.

"Grace! Can you hear me?" I yelled.

"I hear you. Did you find anything?"

"No."

Another couple of minutes passed. Then I heard Grace scream. I turned in the direction of the noise and ran as fast as I could through the fallen branches and dead vines.

"Grace! I'm coming!" I whistled loudly through my fingers to signal the rest of the searchers that we had found something.

"Oh, no, no, no!" Grace wailed.

My gut turned to ice as I imagined what she must have found. Were they injured? I didn't want to know, I didn't want to see, but I kept moving.

Grace crouched on the ground near the Initial Tree, a large oak presiding over a small clearing near the bridge. Every couple in Crystal Haven had carved their initials there for as long as anyone could remember.

Then I saw what was on the ground.

"Grace!" I ran to her and pulled her away from the tree. A pirate zombie lay at its base, a knife protruding from his ribs.

"Paul! I can't believe it . . ." Grace was crying and alternately clinging to me and trying to go back to where the zombie lay against the tree.

"Grace, stop. I have to check and see if he's . . . if he's okay."

Grace nodded and took a deep breath.

I knelt next to the pirate and forced myself to feel along his neck for a pulse. Nothing. There was so much makeup and fake blood on the costume that I wanted to double-check that the knife was real, but knew I shouldn't touch anything.

I heard crunching through the woods and then Seth's voice.

"Here they are!" Seth said. "What's all the scream-ing about?"

I turned and tried to block Seth's view of his father's body, but what I saw didn't make any sense.

Paul, Sophie, and Mac walked just behind Seth and Alex. Paul was laughing at something Mac had said. Grace turned at the same time I did and then launched herself at Paul.

"You're alive!" she said and threw her arms around him.

Paul staggered backward as the full force of Grace hit him.

He laughed. "Well, I'm a zombie, but I'm alive," he said. She clung to him and he stopped smiling. "What's going on?"

"Seth, take Sophie to Message Circle and get her something to drink," I said. I stayed crouched in front of the zombie in a vain attempt to block their view of the dead man.

"Where are my mom and dad?" I asked.

"They went back to tell Vi we'd found Paul and Sophie," Alex said.

Seth hesitated and then Mac leaned over and said something to Alex. Alex slung his arm over Seth's shoulder and took Sophie's hand.

"I'm pretty sure there are cookies," Alex said, "But we better hurry before your Papa and Nana Rose eat them all," he said.

Seth craned his neck around to see what I was hiding but went with Alex back into the woods.

Mac approached and knelt next to me to examine the body.

Grace continued to cling to Paul and they stayed back away from the tree.

"That guy's in a pirate costume just like mine," Paul said. His voice cracked and I saw him pull Grace tighter.

"I thought it was you when we found him here," Grace said. She sniffled and buried her face in Paul's chest.

I signaled to Paul that they should step farther away from the body. He nodded and pulled Grace away from the clearing toward the path that led to Message Circle. I felt Paul's eyes on me as he comforted Grace.

Mac leaned forward to look into the face of the dead man. "Who is it? I can't tell with all the makeup."

My old police training kicked in and I scanned the scene for clues. Even though I had never worked homicide, I knew that even a small detail could be important.

The pirate costume was remarkably similar to Paul's. He wore knee-high brown suede boots, with gray ripped pants tucked into them. A formerly white shirt with long cuffs peaked from under a jacquard vest and a long coat with a row of buttons running down the front. A red sash held a fake pistol and small sack of treasure. His hair was long and matted and he had worn a red bandanna under a three-cornered hat. His plastic sword lay next to him among the moss and leaves.

I noticed his left hand and my breath caught.

He wore a large signet ring on his middle finger. I bent to examine the ring—gold with the initials "DEV." I hadn't seen it in fifteen years, but Derek had worn it as long as I had known him.

I cleared my throat. "I know who this is." I pointed to the ring and lowered my voice so only Mac could hear me. "I think it's Derek Vaughn."

Mac puffed out air. "Will you take Grace and Paul back to Message Circle and send Tom Andrews and Charla this way? Tell them to call the medical examiner."

I left Mac crouched by the body and walked to where Paul and Grace stood huddled together.

"Did you know there was another pirate?" Grace asked Paul.

He shook his head. "I only saw our team of zombies. I didn't really pay any attention—all the costumes were pretty gory."

"What if *you* were supposed to be the dead pirate?" Grace asked.

10

Mac stood and held his hands up as he walked toward us.

"Grace, we don't know anything about this yet," he said. "Don't jump to conclusions, and please, both of you, don't talk to anyone about what you've seen here."

Paul nodded agreement and tightened his hold on Grace. She wiped her eyes with her T-shirt and took a deep breath.

"Let's go check on the kids and I'll send Tom and Charla here to help Mac," I said.

We crunched through the leaves along the makeshift trail that led from the bridge to Message Circle.

"We'll have to leave as soon as possible," Grace

said. "I had hoped to have the whole weekend to spend with Seth and Sophie before . . ." She turned her head into Paul's shoulder.

"No one is going anywhere tonight," Paul said. His arm was tight across Grace's shoulders. "We don't even know how the pirate died. Maybe he had a heart attack."

Grace pulled away from him. "There was a knife sticking out of his chest. I'm sure his heart stopped when the blade sliced into it."

Paul took a deep breath and let it out.

"Lots of zombies had fake knives as part of their costume," Paul said in what I was beginning to realize was his Grace-calming tone.

"He's right, Grace," I said. "I couldn't tell in the dark if the knife was real or not. Maybe this wasn't murder." I didn't believe that. The knife looked pretty vicious to me. But Grace needed to pull herself together before we got back to the group or she'd cause a panic. She was just like my mother—you could never tell whether she was going to freak out or lead her troops into battle. Grace was in freak-out mode right now.

The celebrating was still going strong back at Message Circle. Vi approached as we entered the clearing.

"What's going on?" Vi asked. "The kids said someone was hurt? We have to be onstage in three minutes."

The costume contest was in full swing. Each team was allowed to enter two members for the contest and Vi had elected herself and Paul as representatives.

"Mac is dealing with it, Vi, don't worry," I said.

"Who is it? I haven't noticed anyone missing besides Paul and Sophie earlier."

I shook my head and tried to give her a quelling stare.

"I have to find Charla and Tom," I said. "Mac needs their help."

Vi grabbed my arm and pulled me away from Grace and Paul.

"Did you find another murder victim?" she asked.

I took a deep breath and reflected that this was, unfortunately, not a crazy question.

"I don't know yet," I shrugged her hand off my arm. "He was dressed as a zombie and we have to wait for the medical examiner to tell us what happened, but whoever it is, he *is* dead. You need to keep this quiet for now until we know more."

Only the costume contest stopped her from quizzing me further. She grabbed Paul's arm and pulled him toward the center of the circle where the judges waited.

I pushed my way through the crowd, scanning for Tom. He was taller than Charla and I figured I might be able spot him more easily. I finally found him by the cookies with Seth and Sophie.

"What's this about someone hurt in the woods?" he asked.

"Mac needs you and Charla to help him. Do you know where she is?"

Tom nodded and stuffed the rest of his cookie in his mouth. He pointed to the front of the crowd that was watching the zombies parade in their costumes.

I turned to the kids. "Your mom is over there by the back row of benches. Why don't you go sit with her while Tom and I help Mac? And please, don't talk to anyone else about the man in the woods. We don't want a bunch of people showing up or worrying."

Seth took Sophie's hand and they skirted around the crowd. Tom and I approached Charla and I quietly filled her in on the situation. The three of us headed back into the woods.

Mac stood guard over the body as we approached the tree. Charla had called the medical examiner on our way to the bridge.

"Who do you think it is?" asked Tom.

Mac shook his head. "I can't tell for sure with all the makeup on and there were so many visitors, it might be someone we don't even know. But Clyde thinks it's Derek Vaughn."

"How can you tell through all the makeup?" Charla asked.

I pointed at his hand. "That's his ring."

Tom and Charla turned to look at the body.

Tom knelt next to the zombie.

"Don't touch him, Andrews," Mac said.

Tom's shoulders tensed. "I *know*," Tom said.

"We'll need to send him for an autopsy and collect what we can from around the body," Mac said. "When the crime scene team gets here we'll rope off the area. It's going to be a long night."

Mac drew me aside. "You should go keep an eye on Grace. She seemed pretty shaken up. If she didn't already know who this was, it's only going to be worse for her when she finds out. I'll be home as soon as I can."

"What do you mean? Of course she doesn't know."

Mac held my gaze for a moment and then looked away. "You said she got very close to the body when she thought it was Paul. She had makeup on her hands and face. And she used to be engaged to the guy. Maybe she already knows."

I opened my mouth to argue and then stopped. Mac was right. Grace could just as easily have seen the ring as I had. She had been kneeling over the body. Maybe she did know. But why would she pretend she didn't?

I didn't want to leave the scene, but knew there was nothing I could do to help them and Grace would certainly require some support when she found out it was Derek. *If* it was news to her.

I walked back through the woods to Message Circle where the costume contest was finishing up. I got to the circle just in time to see Mayor Winchester hand the trophy to Vi. What a relief. If she hadn't won, we never would have heard the end of it. As it was, she was going to be insufferable, but at least she wouldn't seek revenge against anyone who beat her.

I saw Grace through the crowd and she spotted me at the same time. She pushed her way through zombies and runners, dragging Paul behind her.

"What's going on out there?" she asked. "Do they know who it is?"

I shook my head, deciding it would be better to wait for confirmation before telling her about Derek.

Grace turned to Paul. "We're going to have to tell her."

11

❦

"Tell me what?" I said and regarded them both with narrowed eyes. *Did* they already know it was Derek?

Paul looked down at his tall brown boots that matched the ones on the dead body in every way. As I examined him, I agreed that the costume was identical. I remembered that they had cobbled together a costume quickly after they arrived. I thought Vi had said she sent them to the costume shop in Grand Rapids. It would be something to look into.

"We saw a couple of men following us this morning," Grace said. "After we left Rupert's office, we noticed them and instead of going home, we went to the marina just to see what they would do. There were a bunch of people there and we figured they wouldn't try anything with so many witnesses."

"I saw them," I said. "But they went into Alex's restaurant. They didn't follow you."

"We think they realized we'd seen them and decided to back off," Paul said.

"But we saw them again just before the race started," Grace said. "They were loitering in the parking lot. I know they saw Paul in his costume." Her voice rose and I saw her take a breath. She lowered her voice and continued. "They absolutely would have known he was the pirate."

Paul put an arm around her shoulders and pulled her close.

"What happened to you, Paul?" I said. "We were worried when you didn't show up with the rest of Vi's team."

He glanced sheepishly at Grace. "Yeah, I've already heard about the search party. Sophie had to use the bathroom and the only one I knew of was back at the parking lot. I meant to call Grace to let her know, but my phone had fallen out of my pocket. These costume pants are really loose and the pockets are shallow. By the time we'd walked to the bathroom and back, and I had located my phone, Mac and Seth found us and said everyone was out looking for us."

"Where did you get the costume?" I asked.

Paul shrugged. "Some costume shop in Grand Rapids. Vi drove us there yesterday afternoon."

Grace pulled her arms across her chest and shivered. "How did that other person get the same costume as Paul?"

"I'm sure that's a question that the police will be

asking as well. You two should take the kids and go back to the house," I said. I studied the crowd for Seth and Sophie. Grace's fears fed my own. What if the killer did mean to attack Paul? As I ruminated on their concerns, the bonfire and torches cast menacing shadows on the woods, and the zombie makeup on half of the crowd made me nervous.

I spotted Seth talking to Alex and Diana. The three of us pushed our way through the throng. The crowd was getting rowdy now that the contest was over. Laughter and snippets of conversation floated around us. Zombies and runners stood together discussing the race.

I reached Seth and told him it was time to head out just as a sudden hush fell over the clearing.

Flashing lights shone in the distance through the trees and two men with a stretcher came along the path. I saw Tom Andrews approach them and point them in the direction of the bridge and the body.

Questions began immediately.

"Has someone been hurt?"

"What's going on?"

Charla approached Mayor Winchester and whispered something in his ear. His shoulders slumped and he handed Charla the microphone he'd used to announce the winners of the costume contest.

Zombies and runners turned in her direction.

"There's been an . . . accident in the woods," she began. She held up her hand to halt the questions. "We'll need everyone to cooperate by staying calm while we try to gather some information."

This caused more muttering and people continued to shout questions.

"Is the Vaughn Jewelry's zombie team still here?" Charla asked.

The crowd parted as five zombies came forward. I recognized Tatiana's pale blonde hair and wondered why she was on the Vaughn team. Even with makeup on, Logan's black swoop of gelled hair stood out. I assumed the other three were Logan's parents and Theo Lancaster. Richard and Nora Vaughn, dressed like normal people, joined the crowd of zombies.

Charla handed the microphone to the mayor and stepped off to the side with the Vaughn team.

I wanted to follow them to hear what they would say but Vi and Sophie and then Mom and Dad stopped me before I had a chance to sneak away.

"What's going on?" Dad asked.

"One of the zombies has been hurt in the woods," I said.

"Oh, my," Mom said. "Who is it?"

"It's hard to tell with all the makeup," I said.

"Can't you just ask?"

I shook my head and looked at the ground.

Mom held her hand to her mouth and her eyes grew huge. "Is it a dead zombie?"

"I think that's redundant," Vi said.

Mom and I both glared at her.

"Shh!" I said.

Just as I shushed Vi, a keening wail came from the Vaughn zombie crew.

We turned to see who was making the noise. Richard

Vaughn held his wife, Nora, while she cried. The rest of the Vaughn Jewelry zombie team stood awkwardly huddled together while Nora sobbed.

Charla looked uncomfortable and tried to calm her.

"I want to see him!" Nora said.

Charla was shaking her head and talking quietly. I was surprised Charla had told them about Derek. We didn't have a positive ID, just my memory of his signet ring. But then, I was sure they'd noticed, as I had, that Derek was missing from the crowd.

Grace turned to me. "Is it one of the Vaughns?"

I nodded. "I think it's Derek," I said.

Mom and Grace gasped at the same time and each placed a hand on her chest.

"But he was dressed like a pirate and covered in makeup," Grace said. "I thought it was Paul. How could you tell who it was?" She grabbed my hand and her fingers felt like ice. Her pale face looked skeletal in the dancing light from the bonfire, her huge eyes taking up most of her face.

"I saw his ring. The one with his initials."

Mom and Grace nodded slowly, probably remembering the ring.

"Poor Nora," Mom breathed. She wiped at her cheek.

Dad put an arm around her shoulders and pulled her closer. They didn't know that I knew Mom's secret. Neila Whittle had predicted that mom would attend the funeral of one of her children back when Grace and I were kids. Any mother losing a child hit her particularly hard.

"I have to go say something." Mom pushed away from Dad.

Vi stepped forward and took her arm. "You're the last person she's going to want to see right now. Just leave her to her family, Rose. There's nothing you can do."

Mom looked at Vi as if she wasn't sure who she was, then she shook her head and nodded. "Of course, you're right, Vi. I just feel awful for all of them. Derek was so . . . charming." She looked at Grace and then at me. "I can't imagine . . ."

I glanced over the crowd while Mom had her moment, and saw that Tom was working his way through the group with a clipboard. He seemed to be checking names off on a list. Mac must have told him to be sure he had contact info for the whole group.

The excited and celebratory mood had dissolved. Runners and zombies gathered their belongings and straggled toward the parking lots. The runners had all parked in the south lot, while the zombies and the organizers had parked in the middle lot closest to Message Circle.

I turned to Seth and Sophie. "We should get you two home to bed."

"Of course," Paul said. "Let's all go home." He steered Grace toward the parking lot.

"Shouldn't we stay and help Mac?" Vi said.

The last thing Mac would want right now was deputy Vi.

I shook my head. "We'd only get in the way, Vi. The best thing we can do is to help Tom clear the area and make sure he has everyone's contact info."

"You can do that." She waved her hand at me in a

shooing gesture. "I'm not good at the boring paper-work."

I sighed. "Okay, you head home with Mom and Dad."

I stopped to talk to Tom, but he said he had every-thing under control since Charla was also there col-lecting names and addresses. He reached into his pocket and pulled out Mac's keys.

"Mac said he can catch a ride with me or Charla later." He dropped the keys onto my palm. He tilted his head and gave me an understanding look. He knew that even though I hadn't returned to police work, it was hard for me to walk away from a suspicious death.

I trudged into the trees alone.

Our 5K course had meandered through the woods, but the main path back to the parking lot was less than a mile. As I walked farther from the bonfire and the murmur of voices in Message Circle, my thoughts turned to Derek Vaughn and who would have wanted to kill him.

I hadn't seen him in years, but the Derek I had known was friendly and charming, and I couldn't imagine anyone wanting to kill him. He wasn't perfect, and he'd probably left some jealous boyfriends in his wake, but murder? I'd also heard rumors over the years—mostly from Vi—that he had moved to Chi-cago and that his gambling problem had nearly bank-rupted his father when he bailed Derek out. But that had been years ago and as far as I knew Vaughn Jew-elry was doing well. I wondered why he had come back this weekend. He couldn't possibly have known that

Grace would be here. *I* didn't even know Grace would be here until a couple of hours before she arrived. Then I thought of Grace and her worry about Paul. Was it possible that Derek *had* been confused for Paul and it could have been Grace's husband, Seth and Sophie's dad, sitting out there under a tree with a knife in his chest?

12

❦

At five a.m. Saturday morning, I finally got out of bed. I'd hardly slept and Mac had not returned home. With both dogs and Seth staying at my Mom's, the house felt empty and cold.

I had just pushed the button on the coffeemaker when a car pulled up outside. I went to the front window and looked out. A police cruiser idled in the driveway with Charla behind the wheel. Mac climbed out of the car, waved to Charla, and slowly mounted the steps to the porch.

I swung the door open before he reached it. His eyes looked tired and worried, but he smiled and pulled me into a hug. I quietly steered him toward the kitchen and we sat at the small table.

After he had gulped down half a mug of coffee, I felt comfortable quizzing him.

"Was it Derek?" I asked.

Mac nodded and rested his chin on his hand. "I just came from the Vaughns' house. They were expecting it, but it was still horrible. I hate that part of the job."

I put my hand over his and waited.

"I suppose it's a good thing, though. It makes me even more motivated to find the killer when I spend time with the family left behind."

"Any leads yet?"

"As you saw, he was stabbed and it's the likely cause of death. There were signs of a fight and some defensive wounds. I don't expect any surprises but the official report won't come through until early next week. No witnesses have come forward, so we'll need to interview everyone involved with the zombie run and try to piece together his last hours."

"Can I help?"

Mac shook his head. "I'm going to try to sleep for an hour or so—I'm meeting the team at eight to discuss what we know and plan the next steps."

He slowly mounted the stairs and then I heard him overhead. First one shoe, then the other clunked onto the floor, and then the house was silent. Mac had perfected the ability to fall asleep quickly, even if he was stressed or worried. I envied the skill. It seemed the slightest thing could set my brain racing, especially when I was overtired.

Not a morning person, I was surprised at how loud the birds were at this early hour. Did I usually sleep through all this noise? I puttered in the kitchen, not wanting to disturb Mac. Unlike him, my brain was still in overdrive from my night of tossing and turning. I couldn't shake the feeling that Grace was involved somehow. She herself was worried that the murder had been meant for Paul, and I didn't like the coincidence that she and Derek had both returned to Crystal Haven after so many years away on the very same weekend.

I had picked up the house and was just contemplating going for my morning run when I realized I didn't have to train anymore. I was at a loss. No wonder I usually slept in.

The imperious knock on the door startled me and I rushed to answer it before whoever it was woke Mac. I glanced at my watch—seven o'clock. No one ever came to my door at seven in the morning.

I turned the knob and before I had even opened the door a couple of inches, Lloyd began scolding me.

"I *said* the zombie run would be bad for Crystal Haven and now look at what happened." He pushed the door open and stepped inside, still talking at full volume. "What are we going to do?"

"Lloyd, keep your voice down," I said, frowning at him. "Mac is trying to get some sleep before he has to go back to work and figure out what happened."

Lloyd made a dismissive noise. "How can he sleep when the reputation of Crystal Haven is spiraling downward?!"

I rubbed my forehead. "What?"

"It was bad enough that we've already had two murders in the past year, but this one will put us over the edge. Zombies *and* murders! We'll scare the tourists away."

I refrained from pointing out that, unfortunately, it might actually draw more people to town. It certainly hadn't deterred the tourist trade so far.

"Harriet had the nerve to suggest we cancel the reenactment!" Lloyd said.

I felt like I had missed part of the conversation.

"What?"

Lloyd tilted his head and glowered at me. "Do try to keep up, Clyde. She thinks that it would be in poor taste to hold the reenactment after the murder. I think it's *exactly* what we need. We have to rinse the taint of murder off of our town and the best way to do it is to continue on as we had planned."

"Okay, why are you telling me?"

Lloyd put his hands on his hips. "You and your aunt clearly have a contingent of voters in your back pocket and I know Jillian Andrews has been 'involved' with Mayor Winchester for years. If you and Violet set your mind to it, you can convince everyone to participate."

Ah, now I understood. He wanted to be sure he wouldn't have any opposition now that there was dissent in his own home.

"I don't see any reason to change the Founder's Day plans, Lloyd. D—the victim wasn't from Crystal Haven."

"Do you know who it was, then?"

"I do, but I don't think it's public knowledge yet. I'm sure the police will make an announcement later today."

"I hope it's before noon. The parade starts at one o'clock."

His concern for the dead was underwhelming but I refrained from mentioning it in the hopes he would leave.

I shrugged. "I think you should carry on as if there won't be any changes to the schedule."

"Thank you, Clyde." He grabbed my hand and shook it. "I'm so glad you see things my way." I thought that was taking things a bit far, but he seemed to be preparing to depart, so I didn't argue.

"I'll let you know if I hear anything that will impact your plans." I pulled the door open and pointedly waited.

He nodded and stepped onto the porch. I swung the door to close it and he turned back toward me.

"Can I send Harriet over if she still thinks we should cancel? I'm sure she'll listen to you."

Again, I was shocked into silence. I just nodded and clicked the door shut. I leaned against it and took a deep breath.

Mac lumbered down the stairs a few moments later looking rumpled and just as tired as before his brief nap.

"Coffee?" he asked.

"It's the same stuff from earlier. We can make a fresh pot . . ."

He waved off the suggestion and headed to the kitchen.

"This is better. The bitterness will wake me up."

I shivered a bit as he poured the thick dark brew into a cup. But Mac put enough sugar and cream in his coffee to pass as dessert anyway, so maybe he could tolerate it.

"I'll take a quick shower and head back in to the department," he said after several long sips.

"Lloyd was just here," I said.

He quirked an eyebrow. "I thought I heard you talking to someone. What was *he* doing here so early?"

"He wanted an update on the events at the zombie run, to remind me he had always thought it was a bad idea, and to ask for my help in lobbying not to cancel the Founder's Day celebration. In that order."

Mac set his mug on the counter and leaned against the sink. "I forgot all about Founder's Day. We'll have to cordon off the area where Derek was killed and keep the reenactors away."

"You don't think they should cancel?"

Mac snorted. "Does it matter? It will be easier to just guard the crime scene than to try to cancel Founder's Day. Especially if he's got you on his side."

I stepped closer and rested my forehead on his shoulder. "I can't believe we've had another murder. Do you think there could be any truth to what Grace was saying? She's convinced it was meant for Paul."

Mac slipped his arms around my waist. "It's too early to tell. I have to assume the killer knew it was Derek, but after their story the other day, I think you should all stick together if you go to the celebrations. Don't let Grace or Paul wander off alone."

Twenty minutes later Mac was showered and I had tossed on jeans and a sweatshirt. We walked together to the driveway and he kissed me quickly on the forehead. He hopped in his truck to go to work and I climbed into my Jeep to drive to Mom's place. I figured they'd all be awake by now and I could find out what gossip Vi had picked up.

Baxter greeted me with his full complement of moves when I entered the front door. Tail wagging, head butting, drooling, and shoving his head in my bag looking for treats. Even Tuffy seemed glad to see me in his own subdued way.

"Clyde, what took you so long?" Vi said after Baxter had calmed down enough to allow me entrance.

"It's only eight o'clock, Vi." I set my bag down on the hall table.

"We've been up for hours! Grace thinks there's a killer on the loose and he's after her and Paul." Vi grabbed my hand and dragged me to the dining room.

I was surprised Grace had been so forthcoming with her information. She'd acted so secretive when we were at Rupert's.

Mom rushed over to me as I entered the dining room. "Clyde, you have to get Mac to arrange for police protection. Grace and Paul are in danger!"

"I know, Mom. Grace told—"

"Paul and I explained about that unhinged client who lost his savings in the last downturn," Grace interrupted. "He blames us and maybe he's followed us out here."

Ah. So not entirely forthcoming. Nothing about organized crime, the SEC, or the FBI. She'd have my aunt and parents looking for a lone deranged killer instead of several trained assassins. However, if the two men *I* had seen were the trained assassins, I doubted we needed to worry. They were terrible at blending in and seemed a bit lost. I gave Grace my one-raised-eyebrow look. She hated it because she couldn't do it, but I made my point.

"Where are the kids?" Seth was notably absent from a table filled with food. I wondered if he was sick.

"They're playing a game on the computer," Paul said. "We asked Seth to entertain his sister since they haven't seen each other in so long. She misses him."

"We've been making a plan to protect Paul and Grace and to prove to the police that they should guard them until the killer is found."

"How can you be so sure the killer hasn't already found his intended victim?" I asked.

Mom and Grace stared at me with identical looks of pity and disdain.

"Clyde, please," Mom said. "Who would want to hurt Derek? *Every*one loved him. He was a wonderful person. So funny and charming . . ."

I saw Grace's quelling glance at our mother. She flicked her eyes at Paul, who sat tense and pale with hands clasped tightly on the table.

"Of course, people change, I suppose . . ." Mom trailed off. She passed the plate of muffins around to distract us from the tense mood that had settled over the table.

"I think we need to be careful today," Dad said. "Everyone should stick together when we're out in public. No one goes off on their own." I smiled my thanks at him for saying exactly what I was thinking.

"You're right, Frank," Mom said. She plopped a muffin on his plate and patted his shoulder.

"Maybe we shouldn't go to the Founder's Day events," Grace said.

I took a breath to say that that sounded like a great idea.

"Hey, when's the parade?" Sophie bounded into the room with Seth close on her heels.

"Yeah, I want to see how a 'dignified' celebration looks," Seth said, making air quotes.

"I can take them," Dad said.

"Aren't you going?" Sophie turned to Grace.

Grace glanced at Paul and a message must have passed between them.

"Sure, Soph, we can all go," Grace said.

"I heard Mr. Munson wears a wig every year," Sophie said. She giggled and glanced at Seth.

"Well, he feels it's more accurate to the period to have his hair in a ponytail," Mom said.

"I'll bet he just likes the idea of having hair *at all* at least once a year," Seth grumbled. Obviously he had not forgiven Lloyd for trying to cancel the zombie run.

"Are you going to wear a wig, Papa?" Sophie bounced on her toes and I was reminded of Vi.

"No, hon. I don't do that part of the reenactment.

I'm one of the townspeople from Grand Rapids. I have to try to convince Delphine to come back home," Dad said.

"But she doesn't want to because her boyfriend lives here?" Sophie asked.

"Sort of. She and Elwood fell in love, but her family didn't approve and they had to move here to start their own settlement."

"Yeah, Seth told me." Sophie flapped her hand in dismissal. "I hope there isn't any kissing."

"Usually the kissing gets interrupted by the shooting of the cannon," Vi said.

"Ooh, a cannon?" Seth said. "I didn't know about that."

Grace tugged on my sleeve and tilted her head toward the living room.

I followed her out of the room just as Vi launched into the Founder's Day story.

Grace went to the window and looked outside. She hugged herself and sighed.

"What's up?" I asked. I glanced outside as well, but the neighborhood was quiet at this hour.

"I'm sorry to push you on this, but I really need to know if you've had a chance to talk to Mac about the kids."

"Well, he's been a little busy." I crossed my arms. "What with the murder and all."

"I know, of course he has," Grace said. Her eyes filled with tears. "I can't believe Derek is dead. I feel like it's my fault. I never should have come back here."

"Grace, we have no proof that Derek's murder has anything to do with you or Paul. It may not have anything to do with the zombie run at all," I said. "Mac is looking into things, but Derek has been gone for a long time, just like you. There have been rumors that things weren't always great for him in Chicago."

Grace turned from the window to look at me more closely. "What do you mean?"

"I don't really know much, just that there were rumors about gambling and I know that Theo and Aaron have been partners in the jewelry business for years. Didn't Derek always say that's what he was going to do?"

Grace nodded. "He planned to stay here and work for his father's company. It's one of the reasons I was so relieved when you had that dream about New York. It gave me an excuse to leave."

"What?" I said. "What do you mean, an excuse?"

She held my gaze for a moment. "You didn't think I left Crystal Haven just because of your dream, did you?"

"Well, yeah. I did." And blamed myself for it for years.

"Oh, Clyde. Come on," Grace said. "Do you really think I would uproot myself, break up with my perfect fiancé, and flee to New York because of a dream?"

"Well, you certainly managed to lose all of Mom and Dad's money by ignoring your own dream," I said.

She narrowed her eyes and crossed her arms. "I don't have dreams. I see numbers. All the time."

"So why didn't you see them in time to save their money?"

"I did." Grace turned away from me. "You wouldn't understand."

"Try me."

Grace sighed. "You have no idea what it was like when you started showing signs of psychic insight practically before you could walk. Mom and Vi and Grandma Agnes watched me for years and never saw any sign of 'the gift.'" She made quotation marks in the air. "Then you start talking about dreams and feelings . . ."

"You were jealous of *me*?" I had often suspected this, but Grace had never admitted it. "But you were the one . . ."

Grace held her hand up, interrupting me. "When they let me handle the money, I was so thrilled that they trusted me, and they were so excited that it was doing well, I didn't want to mess it up." She turned away from me and leaned her head against the window frame. "I didn't listen to my instincts when I felt I should pull the money out. I didn't know enough about how my . . . talent . . . worked."

I sat on the edge of Mom's couch, knocking a pillow to the floor. I remembered that time—I was only Sophie's age and we were living in what is now my house. Mom and Grace didn't speak for two weeks. Dad and even Vi got involved, but it was finally Grandma who called for a truce. She went for a walk with Mom, and when they returned it had all been decided. We moved in with Grandma, and Grace and Mom went back to their usual, somewhat distant relationship.

"I always thought you did it because you were mad at them," I said.

She turned and came to sit on the chair near me. "I feel like I was mad at everyone back then. I guess my teen years were not as smooth as they could have been." She leaned back in the chair and pulled her hair into a ponytail, then let it drop. "But I didn't do it on purpose. In fact, I've tried to pay them back over the years, but they always refuse."

"I wonder if Mom feels guilty for giving you so much control over the money."

"Maybe."

I stayed silent.

"That's why I say it wasn't just your dream that sent me to New York. You were only fourteen. Seth's age. Would you uproot your whole life based on something Seth thought would happen?"

I couldn't tell her that I probably *would* do just that. Seth's abilities were uncanny, but usually centered on animals, so it wasn't likely he'd ever see anything that would cause me to run away to another state. Either way, Grace didn't know that Seth had any abilities.

I shook my head.

"In the end, you were right." She shrugged. "I did meet Paul within a month of moving there. But I left in the first place to get away from Crystal Haven and . . . all of this." She waved her hand to encompass the room and the world outside. "Thank goodness my kids haven't shown any abilities. Maybe they can be normal."

I couldn't really blame her. I had left Crystal Haven at about the same age, for similar reasons, but I *could* blame her for letting me think it was my fault for all those years.

"Why didn't you tell me?" I said. My voice had jumped up an octave and I struggled to bring it back into a calm range. "I thought it was my fault you left." I turned away from her. I hadn't intended to have this conversation with her. I certainly didn't want her to know how much I had missed her. She'd see it as a weakness.

"Oh, please," she said. "I'm sure you really hated all the attention as the only useful child."

Many responses came to mind, but all of them would only escalate this argument. I decided to change the subject, a patented Rose Fortune technique.

"What about Derek?"

"Yeah, I had to get away from him as well."

I felt my eyebrows twitch upward at that remark. I opened my mouth to ask what she meant.

"Mom!" Seth came into the room. "Papa thinks we could be reenactors! Can we go?"

I saw her shoulders relax at his interruption. "What? All of us?" Grace asked.

"Well, I think he meant me and Sophie, but I'm sure you and Dad could find a spot, too."

"No. That's okay," she said. "You guys go ahead. Will you be in the parade, then?"

"I think so. That's why Sophie wants to do it." Seth came closer and lowered his voice. "She thinks it's going to be like the Macy's Thanksgiving Day Parade or something. I didn't know how to tell her it's not even close. Maybe if she's in the parade she won't notice. Or at least not as much."

13

~⦿~

We pulled into the gravel drive of the animal rescue league at nine thirty and easily found a spot in the nearly empty lot.

Seth led Sophie inside in full tour-guide mode.

"Are there kittens?" Sophie asked.

"Almost always," Seth said.

I hung back to let them have some time together. When I swung the door open, I saw Seth already talking to his friend Logan Vaughn. Yet again, his dark hair reminded me of the swoop of an ice cream cone.

Theo Lancaster nodded at Seth and pushed away from the wall to come talk to me. I was struck again at how much he had changed from the gawky young man I had known.

There was a confidence in the way he carried

himself that I didn't remember from when we were younger. I had mostly seen him as Derek's shadow— never doing anything without Derek's approval, always just following him around. But a lot of people paled when exposed to the glitter of Derek's personality.

"Hi, Clyde," he said.

"Theo. How are you?"

He glanced at Logan, who had joined the tour to show Sophie all of the animals.

"Been better, I guess. This . . . situation . . . with Derek has the whole family upside down."

He spoke as if it was his own family that was dealing with Derek's death.

"I feel terrible for his parents," I said.

Theo nodded. "Aaron and Derek never got along that great, but it's still a shock. I told Logan I'd bring him over here to get away from the house and let his parents and grandparents make arrangements."

"Did Logan know Derek very well?"

Theo watched the kids moving from kennel to kennel. "I don't think so. Derek didn't come back home all that often, but you know how he was. He always charmed the kids, always sent the biggest presents at Christmas and birthdays—when he remembered at all . . ."

Theo caught my eye and looked away.

"Have you seen much of him lately? You were close back when Grace and Derek dated."

Theo shook his head. "Not really. He had his life and I had mine." He looked away from me to study Seth and Sophie. "How is your sister? Her kids look just like her. The girl is going to be just as stunning as her mother."

I tilted my head at him but he continued to watch the kids. "She's fine. I think shocked, like everyone else who knew Derek."

"We were really close once," he said. "I was sorry to see her leave Crystal Haven."

"I remember. It was always Grace, Derek, and you."

"I actually introduced them." He looked past me, remembering. "Tell her . . . well, tell her I'm sorry about Derek."

Francine, the shelter manager, came through the back door carrying a large bag of dog food over her shoulder. Theo hurried to help her and I got the sense he was just as happy to conclude our conversation as I was.

Francine nodded hello to me and turned to look for Seth.

"Hey, Seth, who's your friend?" she asked.

Seth introduced Sophie to Francine.

"Do you like cats, Sophie?"

Sophie nodded, eyes large.

"Let's let Seth and Logan do their work and I'll show you a new litter of kittens that just came in."

Within minutes Sophie was on the floor with five kittens climbing all over her. Seth and Logan shifted dogs from one kennel to another to clean the empty ones. They filled water and food bowls, and let the dogs out into the exercise run.

Francine roped Theo and me into bathing a couple of new arrivals, and the next two hours flew by in a rush of shared activity.

We got back to the house just in time for the kids to change into their early-townspeople costumes and head off to the parade starting point with Dad. The rest of us were supposed to get a spot in front of Diana's store to cheer them on.

After the strange conversation with Grace that morning, I was hoping to get her alone again to pursue her issues with Derek. I couldn't tell whether she meant she had to get away from Derek for her own reasons, or because she felt she had to actually escape him. If there was more to Derek than I had realized at fourteen—and how could there not be?—I wondered if that something more led to his murder. But Grace avoided me as if she knew that I was now on the hunt for more information about her private life.

Mom smiled warmly at her when she offered to do the dishes with Paul after lunch. Then Grace, the avowed anti-crafter, engaged Vi in a knitting conversation, promising to finally let Vi teach her how to knit. Paul seemed just as surprised as I was and we found ourselves outside with the dogs, tossing a slimy tennis ball for Baxter and a squeaky stuffed toy for Tuffy.

After a few stilted questions on both sides we lapsed into silence.

Never comfortable with Paul anyway, I decided to dial back the politeness. He had asked me to take his children for him, after all.

"Paul, do you really think you and Grace are in danger? I mean, she does have a tendency to dramatize . . ."

Paul threw the toy for Tuffy and it landed on top of the shed where my father kept his tools. Paul sighed and trudged out to the shed to pull it off the top. Tuffy followed, bouncing along at Paul's heels, barking.

When he returned, he stood quietly next to me for a few moments and I thought he had either forgotten my question or, more likely, hoped I wouldn't have the nerve to ask again. I took a breath.

"I think she can be a bit dramatic at times," he said quietly. "But I don't think she's overselling it this time."

Baxter loped up to me and spit his tennis ball at my feet. I picked it up with the tips of my thumb and forefinger and tossed it back into the yard.

Paul turned and looked into my eyes. "We really appreciate what you've done for Seth this year and I think Sophie would be very happy here as well."

"Paul, you're talking like it's a certainty that these men will come after you."

"When I heard it was Derek lying there under the tree, my first thought was that he deserved what he got. I only knew him for a couple of days, but Grace has told me stories." He took a deep breath. "I didn't like him. But then I shifted to the realization that he probably saved me by wearing that costume. No matter how I felt about him, I owe him a debt."

"Mac is still investigating. There are just as many reasons to suspect that Derek had enemies as there are to suspect it was a mistake."

Paul grunted. "Perfect Derek? You must be kidding. Your whole family worshipped him. Didn't you? Grace says you've had a crush on him since you were twelve."

I felt my face growing hot. "Grace doesn't know everything," I said. Great, now I sounded like I *was* twelve. "I did think he was wonderful, *then*. But I'm not harboring any girlhood crush." Plus, I had gotten that feeling when he shook my hand. Not bad, just a warning to stay away.

"Well, I'm glad to hear it. Mac seems like a great guy—"

"Paul?" Grace called through the screen door. "We should go or we'll miss Sophie's big moment."

Both dogs turned at the sound of Grace's voice.

I whistled for them and gestured at the door.

Ears drooped and they walked slowly back to the house.

14

❦

I was surprised to see the sidewalks packed with people. Usually Lloyd had to cajole, threaten, and bribe any straggler to attend, since he'd already done the same to all the participants. I thought that maybe it was leftover zombie run enthusiasts, but there were plenty of new faces in the crowd. The parade only ran along five blocks down the center of town, but the streets were lined four or five deep for the entire length. I had given in to the sad faces and brought the dogs along, and now I was glad for Baxter's large presence. If people didn't move quickly enough, a wet nose went a long way toward convincing them to step aside.

"Oh, my, this is a busy one," Mom said. She stopped every few feet to say hello to a friend or a client. Vi had wisely brought Mom's cards along and she passed them out in her wake to anyone who didn't already know how to find our house and the resident tarot reader. Grace and Paul strolled slowly behind, probably not wanting to be drawn into drumming up business.

I spotted Lucan's red hair as he towered above the crowd and then saw Diana's orange curls next to him. The dogs and I made our way toward them.

Mom, Vi, Grace, and Paul had all fallen behind while the dogs and I wended our way through the crowd and I turned back to look for them. As they drew closer, I realized Vi wasn't *just* passing out Mom's card, which was printed in a restful sage color. The other card was a violent orange. If *my* ears could droop, they would have. I knew what those cards were. With slumped shoulders I continued toward Diana and Lucan.

Vi had been talking up our new business all spring. Ever since she had almost been severely injured in the winter while Mac and I investigated a murder—while we were on vacation—she had decided that I owed her. I had gone from reluctant to recalcitrant to obstructive as the months progressed. Vi had started up a psychic lost and found business, with me as the main attraction. Much of her pet psychic business relied on finding lost pets and dealing with behavior issues, and she continued to perform those tasks. Everything else fell to me. She had set up a fee schedule for everything from lost keys to lost love.

I wish I were kidding.

After the initial flurry of curious townspeople, we hadn't had a huge influx of clients and I had begun to think that it would die a natural death. However, a crowd this size would certainly have a few clients hidden in its depths. I finally reached Lucan and Diana and stood back for the canine greeting. Baxter jumped up and put his paws on Lucan's shoulders—Lucan being the only person who would allow such poor manners—but this always set Tuffy off on a jumping and yipping rampage. A small circle of empty space grew around us.

"What's wrong?" Diana asked, her eyes on me.

"Nothing. Vi is just passing out our business card and I had been hoping that business would taper off."

Diana stood on tiptoe to try to spot Vi. She dropped back onto her heels and shook her head. "I can't see her. But I did see a small clump of people all facing away from the street."

I nodded and turned to control Baxter. If Baxter would get down, Tuffy would stop barking.

"That's her," I said.

"Oh, sorry." Diana shielded her eyes and turned toward the knot of people. "It looks like she's got quite a crowd."

Finished with his Baxter greeting, Lucan followed our gaze up the street. "Maybe she'll drum up something interesting."

My smile faded as I looked beyond Vi's crowd of admirers and saw the two men from the other day. They leaned against the wall between the bookshop and an art gallery. With sunglasses on and arms crossed, they looked like a couple of bouncers at a dance club. I didn't like how close they were to Grace and Paul but they weren't moving and didn't look like they were even aware of my sister or her husband.

"See those guys standing against the wall?" I tilted my head in their direction and Diana and Lucan searched the crowd.

"Yeah, they've been hanging around all week," Diana said. "They came into the store one morning and quickly left when Bethany tried to sell them some protective crystals and a cauldron." Diana giggled. "It's usually pretty obvious when someone has wandered in without realizing what we sell. She likes to really push the witchy aspect when that happens, just to get a reaction."

"What's the matter?" Lucan asked.

"I'm not sure." I shrugged. "Something just doesn't feel right about them." I couldn't tell them about Grace and Paul and their fears.

I was about to turn away when a woman standing a few feet away said, "That's her over there." Her companion turned to look. "Grace Fortune. She and her husband had a huge fight with Derek Vaughn, the murder victim, at the costume shop in Grand Rapids. My cousin works there and she told me . . ."

The women moved further away and had tilted their heads together. I couldn't hear the rest of what they said. Grace and Paul fighting with Derek? Why hadn't they mentioned it and what could they possibly have to fight about?

"Clyde?" Diana shook my arm.

"What? Sorry, I was just thinking . . ."

"I said, here they come." She nodded up the street. I turned quickly, imagining the bouncers striding up behind me, but instead I saw Vi and Mom leading Grace and Paul through the crowd toward us.

"Whew! That was something!" Vi said. "I think I have a couple of new cases for us already!"

"Vi told us about your new business venture," Grace said and she didn't bother to hide her smirk. She knew very well how long I had fought against joining the family business and using any of my talents. Always practical, she never understood why I didn't capitalize on my abilities. In her view it was a lot easier and less dangerous than police work.

"Here they come!" Mom said.

We turned to look up the street at the approaching parade. Lloyd was in front, as usual, leading his group of town settlers all decked out in period dress. One year he had tried to ride a horse, but the next year that got voted down by everyone who had followed behind him. Since then a few more experienced riders took up the rear of the parade.

Seth and Sophie walked together with the settlers group. Someone had found them costumes that looked like something out of *Little House on the Prairie*. Seth wore brown pants tucked into high boots, suspenders, and a wide-brimmed hat. Sophie's dress was too long and dragged a bit in the street. Her bonnet slipped every few steps and she had to shove it back out of her eyes. Cowboys and farmers walked with them.

As I watched them pass, I thought that they were lucky to be in the settlers group, as the townspeople wore everything from Jane Austen-era dresses to Civil War hoop skirts. Lloyd had grown less picky over the years and allowed the reenactors to choose their own costumes. This certainly led to a more interesting parade.

After the settlers and the townspeople passed, the group of early spiritualists appeared. This was not really historically accurate, as the spiritualists came some twenty years after the town was founded by the star-crossed lovers, but there had been a petition a few years earlier stating that if the parade was to be a tourist attraction, we should certainly make it clear that Crystal Haven offered mediums and psychics and had done so for (almost) as long as people had lived here.

The spiritualists, who wore everything from Victorian dresses to gypsy garb, approached and we heard laughter rippling along the crowd. It came in our direction like a wave and I noticed Vi with her hands clasped under her chin and a maniacally gleeful grin on her face. She stood on her toes and then I saw what was causing the excitement. A band of ten or fifteen zombies stumbled down the street. They dragged their legs and groaned horribly at the crowd, who seemed to be thrilled at the new addition to the parade. As the parade slowed for Lloyd to address the spectators up ahead, each group had a small entertainment planned. The zombies broke into a Michael Jackson-esque flash mob and even got some of the audience to join them. I rested my forehead on one open palm and sighed. Lloyd would never, ever let me live this down. The minute he discovered what was happening behind him, he'd know Vi was the ringleader.

The one-minute stop ended and the parade continued its slow crawl up the street. The fire brigade followed the zombies, and then the historical society members. The whole parade only lasted about fifteen minutes and that was because Lloyd set the pace at a slow crawl and had five scheduled stops. The parade ended in the park by the gazebo and after the last horse had passed, the crowd dispersed. We walked the few blocks to the park to pick up Dad and the kids.

"I think it was a pretty good parade this year," Mom said.

I saw Grace roll her eyes at Paul, who suppressed a grin.

"The zombies certainly added a unique element," Grace said to Vi.

"Did you know about that?" I turned on Grace and Mom, who adopted identical innocent-but-not-innocent expressions. "Lloyd is going to have a fit."

"I wish Lloyd would bring back the jugglers," Vi said.

I stopped and glared at her. "I don't think there were any jugglers among the original settlers, Vi," I said. "And there certainly weren't any zombies."

Vi grinned. "I know, but it made for an exciting parade when that guy had the swords and the torches all flying through the air. And at least the zombies knew how to dance."

15

~~♦~~

After the parade, Tom Andrews had asked Grace and Paul to come to the police station to answer some questions. Mac stepped in when Grace questioned Tom's authority and Tom agreed that she probably didn't need to be interviewed. Grace acquiesced to Mac's personal invitation, and the four of them walked to the station. The kids had gone back to my parents' house to change out of their costumes and wait for the reenactment. I gladly went home alone for a brief reprieve from the crowds and my family. I tossed my tea bag in the trash, and prepared to take a sip when I heard a truck rumble to a stop out front. It was late afternoon on Saturday—too late for mail or deliveries. I reluctantly set the mug down on the counter and went to the front window.

A small moving truck had pulled up across the street. The house had been empty since the summer before when its owners had left abruptly. A FOR SALE sign languished on the lawn, and since everyone knew who owned the house, I had never seen anyone even stop to take a flyer out of the box.

The movers rolled the door open and flipped the ramp onto the street with a loud crash. Shouting and banging commenced as furniture paraded out of the truck and into the house.

There went my quiet hour before the rest of the Founder's Day celebrations. I retrieved my mug of tea and stood in the window to watch. Vi would have been outside interviewing the movers and checking to see if there was any sign of a dog or cat who could give her more information on the new neighbors. I decided to wait and see who turned up. Whoever it was couldn't be worse than the previous owners.

A beat-up, lime-green, ancient Mustang convertible, unhindered by a muffler, rounded the corner with enough speed to squeal the tires and pulled to a shrieking stop in front of the house. Long silky blonde hair emerged from the driver's side. She stood and turned in my direction—Tatiana. Great. I'd know everything there was to know about the lines on my palms.

She glanced up and down the street and smiled. Then she turned those bright green eyes directly on me and waved. I fought the urge to step back from the window, but since I had already been spotted, I raised a hand in greeting.

She gestured that I should come outside. Gulping

down the last of my tea, I walked to the front door and stepped outside.

"Well, hello, neighbor!" she exclaimed as soon as the door shut behind me.

She crossed the street and met me in my front yard.

"Tatiana, hello. This is quite a surprise," I said. "I didn't even know that the house had sold."

"It hasn't, actually. My cousin, Tanya, knows the owner, and she talked him into renting the place to me for a few months while I decide what I'm going to do. Honestly, I think he was just relieved to have someone move in after all the trouble." She lowered her voice. "I'm sure you know all about it, being neighbors and all."

I nodded that I knew all about it and changed the subject.

"Do you think you'll be moving to town permanently, then?"

She shrugged. "Maybe you can tell my future. With your eyes, I imagine you know a lot of things. I'll trade . . ." She held her hand out, palm up.

I put my hands behind my back. "I'm not really in the fortune-telling business."

"Pity." She tilted her head and seemed to be sizing up my psychic abilities.

"I saw you with the Vaughn family the other night at the zombie run," I said. "Are you very close with them?"

She watched the movers passing boxes off of the truck. "Not really. My boyfriend is Theo Lancaster. He works with Aaron Vaughn. Theo is devastated over Derek's death—they used to be very close." She dabbed at her eyes. "We had such fun the night of the zombie run. They all came to my shop to put on the makeup and we had a little party. Derek was . . . very charming."

I studied her profile, but she refused to meet my eyes.

"I know. I knew Theo and Derek when we were younger."

"Yes, I've heard all the stories about Derek and your sister." She crossed her arms and turned back toward me. "It's all so tragic. Lost the love of his life, gambled his share of the family business away, and now he's dead."

"I didn't know about the gambling," I said. A lie, I know, but I wanted to hear what she thought on the subject.

She nodded. "He and Aaron had a big fight that night just before we all left. I heard Aaron talk about gambling and I asked Theo about it later."

"Hello!" Harriet Munson waved from her front stoop and minced her way over the uneven grass to stand with us on the sidewalk. "Welcome! I didn't know the house had sold. It will be so nice to have someone living there again. It's always sad for a neighborhood to have a house sitting empty and uncared for."

She turned to me and in a flat voice said, "Hello." Even though we were neighbors, Harriet had never forgiven me for advising her daughter to pursue her acting career. Harriet still didn't have any grandchildren and it was obvious she thought it was my fault.

Tatiana offered her hand and introduced herself.

"Yes, I've heard you took over Tanya's place. I trust it's going well?" Harriet nudged me with her bony elbow.

"I guess you aren't the newest resident anymore, Clyde. You won't be able to light the bonfire."

The newest resident always lit the bonfire at the Founder's Day celebration. Harriet clearly thought this would be a devastating blow to me.

I made a show of checking my watch. "Tatiana, welcome. Mrs. Munson, I'll see you tonight at the reenactment." They both nodded politely and I turned back toward my house.

As I mounted the steps, Mac's pickup truck rumbled around the corner and pulled to a stop in the driveway. He climbed out slowly and I noticed his limp was more pronounced—a sure sign of stress and fatigue.

He raised a hand to Harriet and Tatiana. His face relaxed when he saw me standing on the porch. He walked quickly up the steps to meet me. I swung the door shut behind us, and caught a glimpse of Tatiana and Harriet, both turned toward my house, watching.

"Long day?" I said as I turned back toward Mac.

He nodded and kissed me on the cheek before moving to the living room to sink into the couch.

"What's going on out there?" he asked.

"A palm reader is moving in," I said. "She's quite aggressive—you might want to start wearing gloves."

He smiled but it didn't reach his eyes.

"Is the case not going well?"

"I just spent an hour interviewing your sister and her husband," he sighed. "I'm beginning to understand why you have such a complicated relationship with her."

"I hope she was more forthcoming with you than she's ever been with me."

"I'm not sure about that," he said. "It's like she's on constant high alert. It must be this business in New York that has her so edgy."

"Hmm." I didn't want to get into a dissection of Grace's personality right then, or maybe ever. "Any leads from the other interviews?"

"This will be a tough one, I think," Mac said. "According to the family and everyone we've interviewed, Derek Vaughn was a great guy and no one would want to harm him." Mac shook his head and sighed. "He seemed a bit too slick to me . . . "

Derek wasn't as perfect as his family wanted to claim, but a brief shiver of apprehension went through me. Could Grace be right? Was it a mistake? Was Paul really the intended victim?

"No clues from the knife that killed him?"

"Maybe," Mac said. He rubbed his unshaven jaw, making a raspy sound. "It was one of those fancy knives with carvings like Diana has in her store. Tom Andrews went to see if she recognizes it and has any record of who bought it."

Something tugged at the back of my mind. Had Diana said something about selling an athame? I couldn't remember.

"She's not the only one who sells those—"

Mac held up a hand. "She's not in any trouble. We just thought she could help us trace it back to the owner."

"Have you heard the rumors about the gambling?" I sat down on the chair opposite the couch.

"Gambling?" Mac sat up straight. "Who?"

"I don't remember now where I heard it, probably

Vi told me, and the new neighbor just mentioned it, but Derek had some gambling debts and had to be bailed out by his family. And Theo Lancaster said the two brothers never got along."

Mac sat still for a moment. "No. They didn't share that. I don't know why families try to hide this kind of thing during an investigation. They must know it will all come out eventually and it just makes them look guilty."

"They probably feel like they want to protect his memory."

"I'm sure, but they also might be protecting his killer."

I hesitated to tell Mac about the fight between Paul and Derek at the costume shop. I had no proof and only an overheard snatch of conversation to go on. But wouldn't I be just as guilty as Derek's family if I didn't at least mention it?

"How well do you know Paul?" Mac asked.

I was startled for a moment and wondered if I had spoken aloud. I was about to come to his defense, even though Mac hadn't accused him of anything, when I realized I didn't really know him. He was my sister's husband, and I saw him once a year, if that.

I lifted a shoulder in a noncommittal shrug.

"I only see him at Christmas and even then he's always working. I guess most of what I know about him comes from what Grace tells me."

Mac nodded and then studied his hands in his lap. "We got an anonymous tip that Derek and Paul had a disagreement on Thursday up in Grand Rapids."

I let out a sigh. "I overheard someone talking about

that at the parade, but that's all I know." I held my hands up. "I haven't talked to Grace or Paul about it."

"I don't want to put you in the middle," Mac said, "but when I asked them about it, they downplayed the whole thing. Much different from other descriptions we heard. I guess it's no surprise that the two men wouldn't get along. Everyone in town knows about Grace and Derek and how she left him at the altar."

"It wasn't quite that bad. But they *were* engaged and she *did* leave." I stood and paced to the window. "She's also never returned to tell her side of the story. I think Vi and Mom did a bit of damage control after she left, but it was so long ago I really don't remember the details." What I remembered the most was the guilt I felt after she left. And the feeling of abandonment. After years of adoring Grace, I couldn't believe she would just leave me behind. But she had.

"It probably won't lead anywhere," Mac said. "I'd be willing to bet that whoever killed Derek did it for a much more recent reason. But we will have to pursue it and I'm sure your family will hear about it."

I turned away from the window and sat next to Mac on the couch. "Grace did say something interesting to me yesterday," I said. "She said she *had* to leave Derek. I'm not sure what she meant, and then we were interrupted."

"I was so focused on Paul's fight with Derek, that I didn't really pursue Grace's relationship with him. I'll follow up with her on that."

"I know it's a strange time to be asking this, since you've dragged the parents in for questioning in a murder, but have you thought any more about the kids and the guardianship papers? I think Grace and Paul want to take care of it before they leave next week."

Mac turned to me and took my hand. "I meant what I said. First, I don't think it will ever become an issue. But, if it does, I know you'd want to take them in." He squeezed my hand until I met his eyes. "We're a team. I'm just as attached to Seth as you are and I'm sure I'll feel the same way about Sophie."

I felt my shoulders relax. I just hoped things wouldn't get more complicated after he continued to question them. "Thanks, Mac."

16

❧

"Thank you all for coming tonight to celebrate the beginning of our wonderful village of Crystal Haven," Lloyd said into the microphone. He spread his arms wide to welcome the crowd gathered around the gazebo in the middle of what we all called the town square, but which was actually an acre of grass on the west side of the business section of the city. The torches set up around the area cast jittery shadows over the crowd.

A smattering of applause met his announcement.

"Let's hear the story, Lloyd!" a male voice shouted from the back of the crowd.

"Yeah, move along," another voice chimed in.

Lloyd brought it on himself. Several years ago, after a drunken brawl right in the middle of his Founder's

Day story, he had banned all food and drink until after the ceremony had been completed. It didn't stop people from imbibing at home, but it had cut down on the disorderly behavior. Every year Lloyd bestowed the bonfire lighting honor on Crystal Haven's newest resident. This signaled the beginning of the festivities, which included dancing, roasting marshmallows, and spending time in the food and beer tents. But before the bonfire could be lit, the founder's story had to be told. By Lloyd.

"As many of you know, we come together each year to remember the brave young pioneers who settled here in search of tolerance and acceptance."

This brought some cheering. Those who had heard the story before recognized that Lloyd had shaved about five minutes off his oratory by skipping the history of the westward travelers who were the grandparents of our town founders.

"Delphine Jacobson and Elwood Plotz fell in love during the spring of 1846." One of Harriet's gang stepped forward in an 1850s-era prairie dress and curtseyed for the crowd. She was fifty if she was a day and wasn't pulling off the dewy-eyed youth that the story required. When her lover, played by a portly poker buddy of Lloyd's, took her hand I had to turn away. If I looked at Vi, we would both lose it.

Lloyd continued his story, talking over the giggles and murmurings. "Elwood had purchased the land we stand on today and planned to set up a logging camp. Delphine's father, who was the richest man in Grand Rapids at the time, planned for his daughter to marry into another wealthy family. And if it would be good for business, all the better. His bitter business rival had a son, and the two men, in a moment of rapport, realized the only way to move forward would be to combine their interests. The men shook on the deal and went home to tell their children." Two ancient men shook hands on the gazebo behind Lloyd. They looked as if they could have actually been there when the story was taking place.

"I hope my dad doesn't make *me* marry anyone," Sophie whispered to me.

"But Victor Jacobson didn't count on his daughter's fiery independence," Lloyd waved his fist in the air as if he supported fiery independence. "She refused to participate. He locked her in her room and said she could only come out when she was willing to see reason—or his way of thinking." Delphine was dragged onto the gazebo by her father and he mimed locking her up and pocketing the key.

Sophie gasped and leaned against me.

"Lloyd's really playing it up this year," Vi said in my ear. I still didn't feel safe to look at her, so I just nodded and held my fingers to my mouth. "He must have noticed the zombie run people are still in town spending money in the stores."

"I don't remember the part about locking her up," I whispered back.

"I think he made that up," Vi said.

Lloyd added new facts each year and deleted others. No one in Crystal Haven had any idea what the real story might be.

"Shh!" someone said from in front of us.

Vi glowered at the shusher but remained quiet.

Seth, dressed in his parade costume, climbed over the railing of the gazebo with several other teens and rescued Delphine. They helped her over the barrier to where Elwood waited to whisk her off to his logging camp.

Our group cheered particularly loudly. I wished Grace could have seen it, but she and Paul had been spooked by the two thugs watching them at the parade and had decided to stay home. I suspected they had also had enough of small town quaintness.

I felt a tug on my sleeve.

"I have to go to the bathroom," whispered Sophie.

I nudged Vi and said that we would be right back. I took Sophie's hand and happily turned my back on Lloyd and his newly embellished story of Delphine and Elwood.

The groups behind us shifted as we made our way out of the crowd. I noticed that the fringes were not listening to Lloyd at all and stood in clumps talking quietly and sipping from plastic cups.

Sophie and I made it to the sidewalk surrounding the small park and turned toward the tiny building that housed the public restrooms. Sophie rattled off a constant commentary on the parade and the Founder's Day story, but spoke so quietly I had to bend over to hear her. As we approached the facilities I stood up straight and then stopped abruptly.

The two men who had been following Grace and Paul stood at the edge of the crowd, watching. They didn't seem to be paying any attention to Sophie and me and I was relieved that even if the parents were being followed, the kids seemed to be safe. I wondered when they would realize that Grace and Paul had stayed home.

Sophie stopped as well and waited with the same awareness and patience that Seth often showed.

I squeezed her hand and we continued to the building. I didn't wait outside, but opened the door and checked the room before allowing her to pick a stall. There were only three and all were empty.

"I'll just wait for you here," I said and leaned against the sink.

The men were still there when we exited the restroom.

"I've seen them before," Sophie said to me.

I looked at her in surprise. "Where?"

"They were outside the costume shop when we went to get Dad's pirate costume."

"What were they doing there?"

Sophie shrugged. "Just standing, like they are now. It must be a pretty boring job to just stand around and watch people."

"Why do you think it's their job?"

Sophie smiled and shrugged. "They seem pretty grumpy. Doesn't that mean it's a job?"

I sighed to myself. "Not always, but you're probably right."

"I hope I don't have a job like that when I grow up. I want to do something exciting like talking to animals or telling the future. Like Aunt Vi or Nana Rose."

"Well, I'm sure Nana Rose could teach you about

the tarot when you're a little older. What does your mom say about that?"

I had a pretty good idea what Grace would say. If both of her kids end up with a "useless" talent, she'd be devastated.

"I don't know." She looked at the ground and spoke quietly. "She thinks that stuff is stupid, so I haven't told her. She still thinks I want to be a teacher." Sophie lowered her voice even more. "Which she also thinks is stupid. She says they don't make enough money or get enough respect." She scuffed her feet along the sidewalk and looked down at her shoes.

"Well, I don't think any of those things are stupid," I said. "But you have a lot of time to figure it all out. And you're allowed to change your mind as much as you want."

Sophie looked up and smiled at me.

We made it back to our group just in time for Lloyd's conclusion to the story where Delphine and Elwood run off to the logging camp, get married, and start their own village.

"And so, because of their bravery and love for each other, Crystal Haven was born."

Lloyd raised his hands and took an exuberant bow. The ragged crew of actors stepped forward and took a bow as well. The crowd clapped politely from the front and more enthusiastically from the back. Lloyd had announced earlier there would be no cannon fire tonight since we were in town, and not the woods, like usual. It had been met with booing and hissing and he seemed to want to move quickly to the next stage of the evening.

"This year our ceremonial bonfire will be lit by Tatiana Nettles, our newest resident." Lloyd swung his arm in Tatiana's direction. She turned and waved to the crowd, a huge smile on her face. "She just moved in today and I hope you will all make her feel welcome."

Tatiana took one of the torches and touched the flame to the woodpile in the fire pit. The crowd cheered when it took and a large blaze sprang up.

She walked back to place the torch in its stand and I saw her hesitate. She handed it to Lloyd and melted into the crowd—a breach of protocol. She should have placed it in the stand herself and bowed to the crowd again. Lloyd coached all of his bonfire lighters on the need to give the crowd a good performance. I tried to see what might have spooked her and saw the two men standing by the platform where the torch should go. Theo stood directly in front of them as if he were blocking their path. I was much too far away to hear what he said, but Theo's fists were clenched and his shoulders tensed. The two men stood with feet apart and arms crossed. Even the short one looked like he was glaring down at Theo. They turned and moved into the crowd as Lloyd carried the torch to set it in its spot. Theo pushed his way back into the crowd the same way Tatiana had gone.

No one else seemed to notice. The lighting of the bonfire was always the signal that the party should start and the crowd grew boisterous after the fire erupted. I tried to spot Tatiana's pale hair, but in the dim evening light she had disappeared. Theo had also blended into the crowd and I wondered what the connection could be between Grace's pursuers and Theo Lancaster. Was Grace mistaken? Maybe they weren't after her at all. Maybe this was all about Derek. But, if that was the case, why were they still in Crystal Haven? I was able to locate the two grumpy watchers, as Sophie would call them. They stood sentinel again across the street, arms crossed. Watching. Were they looking for Grace and Paul?

They didn't seem to be paying any attention to our little group and I tried to put them out of my mind. But I held on to Sophie's hand and told Seth to do the same. Vi, Mom, Seth, Sophie, and I discussed which food tent to hit first. It was difficult to hear everyone's choice over the energetic crowd. The smell of wood smoke and popcorn brought back memories of my childhood. I was glad Seth and Sophie got to experience a Crystal Haven event. Lucan and Diana approached, arm in arm. "We're going to head out," she said.

"Okay, I'll see you next week," I said.

"Did Olivia find you?" Diana asked.

I shook my head no. "Olivia Hanson? No, why is she looking for me?"

Olivia was one of the psychics who worked at the Reading Room and was part of Harriet Munson's crowd. I had no idea why she'd be looking for me. Harriet had spread the word about her daughter's lack of a normal life after her meeting with me. In general, her cronies avoided me on the off chance I would ruin their lives as well.

"She says she has to talk to you—tonight," Diana said. "She seemed a little weird about it."

"Thanks, I'll be on the lookout for her," I said.

Lucan waved good-bye and he and Diana walked toward the street. The crowd parted easily in front of them. Lucan had that effect on people.

Vi had been talking urgently with Mom and now turned to me. "If Olivia Hanson is looking for you, you should probably go home."

"What? Why?" I narrowed my eyes at Vi.

"She's all gloom and doom," Vi said. She popped up on her toes to scan the crowd. She barely made it to Seth's shoulder and muttered to herself that she couldn't see Olivia anywhere.

"Can we go get some ice cream now?" Sophie asked. She bounced on her toes and looked like a miniature, younger version of Vi.

We agreed that ice cream sounded like just the right end to the Founder's Day celebrations. Seth led the way toward the Moovalous Ice Cream tent. Vi continued to survey the crowd for Olivia, hands on hips and eyes narrowed. I got in line at the back of our group.

"There you are!" Olivia pushed her way through the ice cream line to reach me. "I thought you'd end up here eventually so I sat right over there waiting." She pointed to the corner of the tent.

Olivia was about my height and at least fifteen years older. She favored brightly colored scarves and noisy jewelry. She reached out to touch my arm and her wrist clanked and tinkled with bangles.

"I had to find you tonight, to warn you," she said. She glanced over her shoulder as if she were about to impart top-secret government information. She noticed

Vi edging in our direction and pulled me outside of the tent.

"What is it, Olivia?" I tried to keep the edge out of my voice, but I was easily irked by the theater that some of the psychics brought to just about every interaction.

"I have a message." She lowered her voice and intoned this news like a Delphic oracle. "It's from your grandmother."

Despite myself, my heart sped up at this announcement. My grandmother had been dead for more than fifteen years. I just as quickly became very skeptical. I couldn't imagine my grandmother choosing someone like Olivia to send a message through after all this time. Why not Neila? Or even me?

As if she read my mind, she leaned toward me and said, "I know I haven't always been very friendly with your family, and I don't know why your grandmother chose me, but I'm just the messenger."

She and Vi had fallen out many years ago when Vi told Olivia that her Siamese cat despised the baby talk way she spoke to him. The interview had ended with Olivia and Mr. Tiddles storming out and a distinct frostiness began.

"Okay, what's the message?" I said.

She cleared her throat and waited a beat to be sure I was paying close attention. "Beware of whom you trust and what you believe," she said.

I waited for her to continue but she appeared so satisfied that I concluded that was it. Grandmother had sent a Chinese cookie fortune to Olivia for her to pass along to me. Great.

"Well, thank you, Olivia," I said. "I'll keep that in mind."

Olivia's face fell. "You aren't going to listen to the warning, are you? I can tell when someone is ignoring a message."

"No. I won't ignore it," I held my hands out in a placating gesture. I didn't want to give her a reason to add me to her list of people to snub. "I just . . . don't know what it means."

"It *is* a bit cryptic," she said. She clasped her hands and set off another round of bracelet clinking. "I'm sorry I don't have anything more concrete, but I can tell you that the *feeling* I got when I received it was very strong. She's extremely worried."

"Thank you for telling me," I said. "I'll be more vigilant in the future."

This seemed to satisfy her and she patted my arm.

"Violet Greer, you are shameless," she said over my shoulder.

I turned to see Vi, her back to us, pretending to eat her ice cream as she crept slowly backward toward Olivia and me.

"Hello, Olivia," Vi said in a flat voice.

"Violet." Olivia's eyes narrowed.

"Thank you, again," I said. "I'd better get my niece and nephew home."

Olivia nodded to me and lifted her chin toward Vi before moving off into the increasingly noisy crowd.

"What'd I tell you?" Vi asked. "Gloom and doom, am I right?"

"No, not really. But it wasn't particularly helpful,

either," I said. "She said Grandma sent me a message to beware of who to trust and who to believe."

"What kind of a message is that?" Vi scowled. "Is she using a Magic 8 Ball these days?"

She put her hands on her hips and glowered at Olivia's retreating figure.

17

The sound of the organ rattles the door as I approach the church. I am alone at the foot of the steps. As I begin to climb they grow steeper and I struggle to ascend as the music becomes louder and resonates deep in my chest.

Finally I mount the last step and reach out to open the door. I notice for the first time that I am wearing black gloves to match my simple, sleeveless dress and shoes. Dread settles in my stomach like a cold stone. I push the door open. There is no one in the church, but at the front a long black box sits on a stand. The sound of the music diminishes as I get closer to the front of the church. Tears blur my vision and I stumble. I grab the back of a pew to get my balance.

I don't want to look in the casket. Afraid to see who is there, I stop a few feet from the coffin and the organ switches its dirge to Amazing Grace. *I take a step forward, and another, feeling as if I am walking through thick, heavy water. One final step. I take a deep breath and look inside.*

Empty.

I run back down the long aisle to the door, past the empty pews. I smell lilies. Their cloying scent reaches out and grabs at my ankles, my hair, my face. I throw myself at the door but it doesn't budge. There is no doorknob or handle, just a smooth gray surface that feels rough, like wood, but cold, like metal. I pound on the door. I try to scream for help but no sound comes out and all the while Amazing Grace *plays on behind me.*

"Clyde! Wake up." Mac's voice reached through the dream and in the misty light of early morning I gasped and realized I was safe, in bed.

"Just a dream," I said. I turned to Mac and curled next to him, shivering.

He made shushing noises and after I assured him I was fine, he fell asleep again. I lay awake, thinking and worrying. I hated these dreams.

I knew it was trying to tell me something, but much like Olivia's message, I had no idea what it meant. Neila had been helping me to interpret the dreams and try to discern whether they were premonitions or just anxieties and worries working themselves out.

I could almost always tell the difference. The predictive dreams left a fuzzy feeling in my brain like a hangover without the headache. This one had left me with the fuzz and a good measure of dread.

I decided to drop in on Neila later in the morning and see if she could help make sense of the dream. I also needed to talk to Grace. The past few days combined with the dream had me worried that maybe Grace was right. Maybe Derek had been killed by mistake.

The clearing around Neila's house was quiet, but I heard the rat-a-tat of a woodpecker farther in the woods and a cardinal calling to its mate. The cottage was nestled far enough into the trees that the smell of earth and old leaves and new life combined into a heady mix.

I raised my hand to knock and the door swung open.

"Hello, dear," Neila said. She smiled up at me from the gray gloom of her entryway. The only room I had ever seen in her house was the warm and cozy kitchen. The rest of the space lay shrouded in shadow. She led me to the back as usual and placed a plate of cookies and a mug of tea in front of me.

"You knew I was coming?" I asked.

Her mouth twitched up at the corners and she lifted a shoulder in a half shrug. "I had a feeling."

She settled herself across the table from me and waited.

I wrapped my fingers around the warmth of the mug. "I had another dream and I need your help."

She nodded encouragement.

I described the dream as well as I could remember it, focusing on the music, the smell of the flowers, the empty casket and my own panic.

As I told her the story, she grew very still and when I told her about *Amazing Grace* following me to the door she went very white.

"Neila? Are you okay?" I stood and rushed to the other side of the table.

Her eyes glazed over and her breaths came quick and shallow. I worried she was having a stroke or a heart attack. Selfishly, I fretted about what I would do if anything happened to her.

She finally focused on my face and patted my hand.

"I'm fine. Just give me a moment."

She sipped her tea and closed her eyes. She seemed to shrink into her pile of shawls.

I stood nervously next to her chair.

"Go, sit." She waved in the direction of my seat.

Neila took a deep breath and let it out. She opened her eyes and looked at me.

"The dream you just described is almost exactly the vision I had all those years ago. The one that sent your mother down the hill and out of my life."

The same hollow, shaky feeling that I associated with my fear of heights spread across my chest. I cleared my throat and tried to focus.

"What part was different?"

"In my vision, I saw your mother in the church and she knew who was in the coffin. *I* just never knew if it was you or your sister." She reached across the table and took my hand. "I still don't know."

I gently pulled my hand away and put it in my lap. Panic rose and I felt dizzy. Recently, if I had a predictive dream, it came true fairly quickly. Neila had predicted that my mother would attend a funeral for one of her children at some point in the future. My dream made it seem that the future was now.

"I was trapped, Neila." My voice shook. I clasped my hands together in my lap to keep them from shaking. "The door felt like wood and metal combined. I couldn't get out and I was alone."

Neila's eyes filled with tears. "That doesn't mean it was your funeral. It may just mean you will *feel* alone. But the other possibility is equally as terrible for your family. It could be Grace's funeral you saw."

I remembered the haunting strains of *Amazing Grace* following me through the church. I thought of Grace's fear that Paul had been the intended victim when Derek was killed.

I stood quickly, shaking the table as I bumped it and causing the tea to slosh over the sides.

"I have to go," I said. I hurried to the front door. I didn't know where I was going, just that I felt trapped and suffocated and had to be outside. I heard Neila shuffling along behind me.

"Clytemnestra," Neila said.

"I'm okay, really," I said. I took her hand. "I'll be

back, I promise. I just need to think. Thank you for telling me about your vision. I hope we're both wrong."

I wrenched open the door and strode to my Jeep. When I looked back at the house, the small gray figure raised a hand and then faded into the dark interior before the door swung closed.

18

Mom: Come quick! We need you!
Seth: Prepare yourself
Vi: I thought you would be here by now.
Dad: 10-96

All four texts greeted me when I picked up my phone from the passenger seat. I sighed. What new drama was happening at my parent's house?

I closed my eyes and took deep, slow breaths. Neila had never specifically described her vision, she only said she had seen that my mother would attend the funeral of one of her children. The prediction had understandably frightened Mom. She had avoided Neila ever since, as if the messenger could somehow cause the message to come true. It also explained why my mother had always pushed me to develop my own talents. She had hoped they could protect me. And she had hated the idea of me becoming a police officer. Between my own dream, Derek's murder—which may have been meant for Paul—and Grace's heightened anxiety, I was starting to think my mother had been justified in her fears. I, on the other hand, would not avoid the messenger.

Still feeling worried and anxious, I maneuvered the Jeep around in Neila's small clearing and drove back down the driveway out to the street. I had promised Mom that Mac and I would come over for dinner tonight. I'd have to evaluate the new urgent situation with my family and decide whether to drag Mac into it.

It only took three minutes to drive to my parents' house. Not quite long enough to calm my racing thoughts. I took a deep breath and pushed my fears into a little box in my mind. I'd deal with it later when I was alone.

My foot had just touched the top step to the porch when the door opened.

"Finally! What took you so long?" Vi said. She had one hand on her hip and the other wielded a finger in a threatening manner.

Baxter pushed past her and wiggled out onto the porch. I rubbed his ears and wished I had Seth's talent, just for a moment, so the dog could tell me what was going on.

"I had some errands and I wasn't checking messages," I said.

"Why do you even have a phone if you aren't going

to check messages?" Vi followed me into the dining room where Mom, Grace, and Paul sat.

I stopped abruptly in the doorway and Vi bumped into me.

"Clyde! I'm so glad you're here." Mom rushed toward me, but I had already spotted the pendulum and the box that held my grandmother's crystal ball.

Grace sat quietly at the table with red-rimmed eyes, leaning into Paul.

"What's going on?" I said. "Where are the kids?"

Seth couldn't resist any form of fortune-telling. He loved the pendulum *and* the crystal ball.

"We didn't want them to hear about our suspicions, so we sent them to the mall with Frank," Paul said.

"What suspicions?" I said.

"We told Mom and Vi everything," Grace said. "About the money and the men who are following us. About Derek and how he was probably killed by mistake."

"You don't know that," I said.

"Mom read my cards," Grace said. "It's all there."

Mom nodded solemnly. "It doesn't look good."

"Paul?" I turned to my brother-in-law. "I can't believe you're going to get all worked up over some tarot cards."

"It's not just the cards," he said. "There's been a threat."

I looked from Mom to Vi and then to Grace.

"What threat?"

Grace took a deep breath. "It was after we left the police station yesterday. There was a black rose on the hood of our car."

I shook my head. "Someone must be playing a joke. No one sends death threats."

"The cards are very clear, Clyde." Mom crossed her arms.

"Okay." I held my hands up. "What are you going to do?"

"We need you to sign those papers," Grace said.

"Of course," I said. "Mac will sign as well, but I don't think they will ever be needed. Should we go see Rupert tomorrow?"

Paul shook his head. "He's coming here in about an hour. He'll notarize the papers and then Grace and I can at least rest easy that the kids will be okay."

I thought it was overly dramatic to drag Rupert here on a Sunday, but the combined anxiety of my mother and my sister were too strong for me to argue against. I wasn't surprised that Dad had taken the kids to the mall. No wonder he'd sent me the 10-96 text. It meant psych patient, but Dad had co-opted it long ago as a "red-alert psychic activity" warning.

"I'll text Mac and make sure he can be here in an hour." I pulled out my phone.

"Wait, before you do that, have you had any . . . visions?" Grace asked.

This was certainly an abrupt change of heart after our last conversation. But I didn't want to tell them about my dream. It would only fan the fire and might push Mom right over the edge.

I shook my head. "No, nothing." I focused on my phone, hoping none of them would pick up on the lie.

"Let's ask the pendulum," Vi said. "You do it, Clyde."

"How many times have you already asked it?" I said.

Vi glanced at the velvet case that held the pendulum, then at Grace. "A few."

That probably meant twenty. Vi was nothing if not persistent with the pendulum when it didn't give her the answer she wanted. I suspected she could browbeat even the pendulum into going along with her plans.

"Mom said you used Grandma's crystal ball last fall and you saw a man who was about to be injured," Grace said.

I nodded, remembering the sick feeling of falling into the crystal's depths and the dizzy spinning as I pulled myself out.

Grace pushed the wooden box toward me. "Would you? Please?" Her eyes were imploring and it brought back memories of childhood antics that always ended in tears.

I took a step back and crossed my arms. While I was committed to learning how to use my psychic abilities, I didn't like scrying. At. All. Theoretically, scrying uses a reflective surface to focus the psychic antenna on the future. Mirrors, shallow bowls of water, and crystal balls have been used for this purpose for centuries. I had even once seen a vision in a bonfire. But the aftermath was rough. Nausea and headache as well as a ferocious hunger seemed to follow what Vi would call a successful session.

"It's too bright right now," I said, clutching at any excuse. "Maybe we can do it later."

"We'll go to my apartment," Vi said. "I have black-out shades in there for when I'm dealing with a nervous client." Vi had converted part of the main floor of the Victorian she shared with my parents into a small apartment with a bedroom, sitting room, and bathroom. She shared the kitchen, even though Mom did all the cooking.

Paul, Grace, Mom, and Vi stood and ushered me down the hallway to Vi's quarters.

Purple walls and a dove-gray couch dominated the room. Decorated in bright, cheerful colors, it was almost as chaotic as Mom's living room, but with less fringe. An orange-and-fuchsia area rug anchored the room and Vi had covered the couch in bright orange, red, and pink pillows. Vi's knitting basket sat next to her rocking chair. Bright balls of yarn spilled over the sides and fell onto the floor. She had four dog beds scattered on the floor of the small space for her animal clients as well as a tall cat maze covered in lime-green carpet. I hoped, for her clients' sakes, that it was true that animals were color-blind.

Mom and Paul sat on the love seat, while Grace folded herself onto one of the larger dog beds. Paul raised his eyebrows in surprise, but Grace's intense expression quieted any commentary. Vi placed the box containing Grandma's crystal on the wooden coffee table and pushed me down onto a soft round ottoman. She hurried over to the window and pulled the shades, sinking the room into a gray gloom.

Mom got up and lit some candles while Vi set a

couple of them on the coffee table. The reflective light from the candles was meant to help the scryer see into the crystal.

Mom settled herself on the couch again and Vi pulled her rocking chair close to the ottoman where I perched uncomfortably.

My knees touched the edge of the table and I reached forward to pull the box closer. It had been worn soft at the edges and corners but the black metal clasp clicked open smoothly. I lifted the lid and carefully removed the clear glass ball with the black velvet that covered it. The small stand nestled underneath, and Vi removed it from the box and placed it in the center of the table.

Mom held out her hand for the ball. I had only used it once in my adult life. After Mom caught Alex, Diana, and me trying to find out who would ask us to the prom, she took the ball and hid it. She had brought it back out last fall during a different investigation.

After buffing the nonexistent fingerprints off of it, she placed it carefully in the stand and surrounded it with the velvet. The purpose of the cloth was to minimize any reflections other than that of the candles and whatever was hidden in the depths of the crystal.

Paul and Grace leaned forward and looked from me to the crystal.

"I don't see anything," Paul said. "Do you?" He turned to Grace.

She shook her head. "I've never seen anything like that. I only get the stock market listings."

Vi shushed them and put her hand on my shoulder.

I closed my eyes and took a deep breath, then opened them and looked deep within the glass. Vi squeezed my shoulder to urge me on.

At first I only saw the flickering candles and their jittery reflections. Then the mist appeared. The smoky haze turned a gray foggy color and swirled inside the ball. The pain started right in the middle of my forehead and a wave of nausea almost made me look away. But I knew it would pass, so I kept my eyes focused on the mist. It felt like a long time. Unlike the pendulum, where you ask it a specific question and in that way control the messages, the crystal always seemed to have its own agenda. *It* would decide what message to give.

I continued to stare at the fog and tried to see past it. Tried to will it to clear and show me its secrets. Vi had stopped squeezing and I was glad to have her comforting hand on my shoulder.

The vapor dispersed and I saw a long alleyway leading into the gloomy distance. A thin figure walked toward me. Blonde hair and a long skirt—I thought at first it was Grace and felt dizzy. But as she got closer, I saw that it wasn't my sister. It was Tatiana and she was crying. She seemed to see me and walked quickly in my direction. She was trying to speak but no sound came out. In my mind I reached out to her, but before I was able to touch her, the fog swirled again and she disappeared. Then I saw a figure lying on the ground. It was wearing the pirate zombie costume but as I got closer, I saw that he wasn't wearing the zombie makeup.

He lay quietly on the ground, not moving, not breathing and when I looked at his face I pulled away from the crystal breaking the vision.

I shook my head to clear it and opened my eyes to the same face—Paul's.

19

―❧❧―

"I knew it!" Vi said. "I knew she'd see something."

"Vi, give her a minute," Mom said. "She looks kind of green."

"Is she okay?" Paul said.

Talking about me as if I weren't there didn't help my mood.

Surprisingly, it was Grace who stepped in to take control.

"Vi, go open the curtains," she said. "Paul, go get her some water, please." Grace turned to me. "Unless you want something stronger?"

I shook my head no.

Mom clasped and unclasped her hands and seemed to vacillate between wanting to stand up or sit down.

When Paul returned with a glass of water, I gratefully drank the whole thing. The four of them hovering and watching me made me feel almost worse than the crystal ball had.

I gestured for them all to sit.

"Well, what was it?"

I decided not to tell them about seeing Paul. I didn't think it would help anyone and I didn't know what it meant yet. That was always my problem with my premonitions. It often took a while to understand them and by then it was too late.

I cleared my throat, which felt dry even after the water. "I saw Tatiana," I said. "She was walking toward me down a dark alley and she was crying."

"Who is Tatiana?" Grace asked.

"Is that the palm reader?" Mom asked. "She took over Tanya's shop?"

I nodded. "She took over the shop and she moved in across the street from me yesterday."

"You guys weren't there, at the Founder's Day evening," Vi said to Paul and Grace. "But Lloyd let her light the bonfire. It's a big honor, but then she disappeared."

"What does she have to do with us?" Paul asked, with an impatient edge to his voice.

"I don't always see what I expect to see and it doesn't always connect directly with my own concerns," I said.

Paul huffed. "Well, that's hardly useful."

I had to agree, but I saw Vi puffing up her chest in preparation for a rant about psychics and their gifts. Grace saw it as well and put her hand on Paul's arm.

Fortunately, the doorbell rang, startling us all.

"That must be Rupert with the papers," Grace said. "We'll get it." She grabbed Paul's hand and dragged him out of the room.

Mom and Vi fussed over the crystal ball and shined it up again before carefully placing it back in its box.

I heard Mac's voice out in the hall and hurried out to talk to him.

I caught the angry look he gave Grace and stopped. "Why would you do that?"

"I merely said that it might be too much to ask of you," Grace said, in that bored tone she used when she didn't want to be questioned. "I thought I was doing you a favor."

Paul turned away from them and I couldn't read his expression.

"I'll thank you to keep your favors to yourself, Grace," Mac said in an icy tone.

I stepped forward to break up whatever was going on.

Mac looked past Grace as I approached. I could tell from the concern in his eyes that they had already told him about our fortune-telling adventures.

"Are you okay?" he stepped forward and drew me into a hug. "I wish they wouldn't make you do these things," he said into my hair.

This was a major step forward for us. It used to be that I would try to hide any psychic experiments from him out of fear that he wouldn't approve and because I thought he was so skeptical that he wouldn't be able to handle it. But I had been wrong to doubt him. It seemed he was a more open-minded skeptic than I had given him credit for. Any disapproval was based in his concern for me, not fear of psychic phenomena.

I was glad he was here and felt myself calming and coming back to my normal self as he held me.

"What did Grace do?" I whispered.

"Grace, why don't you tell Clyde what happened?" Mac turned toward her, keeping his arm firmly around my waist.

"Really, Mac," Grace drawled, "You're overreacting."

"What did you do?" I asked, slowly and with Mom's steely edge to my voice.

Grace sighed and held her hands out to the side. "After Mac talked to us yesterday at the station, I merely suggested to his boss that it might be a conflict of interest for him to be working on the case."

I heard a gasp from behind me. Mom and Vi stepped forward.

"Grace, what were you thinking?"

"Is it really such a big deal?" Paul waded into the argument. "Derek probably had a million enemies. It's not going to be that hard to find the killer."

"Did it ever occur to either one of you that *you* are actually suspects?" Mac said through clenched teeth. "I might have been able to help you. Assuming you didn't do it."

"Okay, that's enough," Vi stepped between Paul and Mac.

I tugged on Mac's sleeve and we stepped out onto the porch. He paced and glowered. I peeked inside to see Grace and Paul in a tense conversation with Vi.

"Mac, we'll figure this out," I said.

He stopped pacing. "You're right," he said. He lowered his voice. "The truth is, Grace is probably right. I shouldn't be on the case. I'm too close to it."

I was surprised he felt that way, but agreed that it would be a lot easier to deal with my sister if my significant other wasn't questioning her in a murder investigation.

"Who's taking over the case?"

"Roy Fisk." Mac said his name with no intonation, but I knew how he felt about Roy. Roy was new to the department, and from the east side of the state. He didn't know the area the way Mac did. He was a strict by-the-book investigator. As long as his boxes were checked, he didn't look any further.

Mac rubbed his jaw and then pulled me into another hug. "Now I know why you were so stressed when you heard she was coming to town. She doesn't pull her punches, does she?"

I shook my head against his chest and wished Grace had never come back to Crystal Haven. "I'm sorry, Mac."

He pulled away and looked down into my eyes. "This is in no way your fault."

"My family is just . . ."

"A handful, but we can deal with it." He smiled and kissed my forehead.

We stepped back inside and Grace looked at us carefully.

"Still friends?" she said to Mac.

"Maybe," he mumbled.

"I knew you wouldn't stay mad," Grace said. She put her hand on Mac's arm but pulled away instantly as if he were hot.

"Let's not fight anymore," Mom said. She was fidgeting with her hands and watching us like she was waiting for an explosion.

"It'll be fine, Mom," I said. I stayed close to Mac and hoped Grace would move on to other subjects.

We were milling uncomfortably around the front door when the bell rang again. Paul swung it open and gestured Rupert inside.

Rupert's light jacket hung askew on his shoulders and his shirt was partly untucked. He had a briefcase and an overstuffed file under one arm.

Grace took his hand and turned her brightest smile on him. "Thank you so much for coming on a Sunday. As soon as I knew you would be here to take care of this I started to relax." She slipped her hand onto his arm in the manner of a Victorian woman being led in to dinner. Rupert gazed adoringly at her.

"Shall we?" Grace swept her arm in the direction of the living room.

Mac took my hand and squeezed. He wasn't going to let this fight affect the issue with the kids.

We settled ourselves on Mom's delicate fringed couches and chairs while Rupert rummaged in his briefcase before he remembered that the papers were in the file he had dropped onto the coffee table.

"All right," he said. "This won't take more than a couple of minutes. Once I find the documents . . ." He flipped through his stack of papers and muttered to himself. "Here they are!" He triumphantly pulled a small stack out of the pile.

He placed the papers on the table and moved the file and his briefcase to the floor.

"This is the new will you asked me to draw up," he said to Grace and Paul. "It has the changes you asked for in regard to the dispersal of your estate in the event of your death."

Paul pulled the paper toward himself. He and Grace read the indicated portion.

"While they are looking that over, you two can read this document that outlines the guardianship agreement and the trust that Mr. and Mrs. Proffit have arranged for the children."

Mac and I signed the paper, Rupert notarized it, and we were done. Grace visibly relaxed after the documents were signed and Rupert began packing up his things.

"Thank you both for doing this," she said.

"It really means a lot to us," Paul said.

"Of course," I said. "We're family and I adore the kids." Mac sat quietly next to me, but I no longer sensed anger in him.

"I know Seth is crazy about you two as well," Grace said. "This will be for the best."

"Let's hope we never need to test it out," I said.

"Of course," Grace said. She didn't meet my eyes. "Let's hope." She reached for Paul's hand.

20

My phone shrilled loudly in the quiet house. I looked at my clock—three a.m. I rummaged on my bedside table to find the phone in the dark. It sat face-down and I grabbed at the thin band of light around its edges.

Mac mumbled and rolled over.

"Hello?"

"Clyde?" Grace's voice sounded staticky. "I'm so sorry."

"What?" I pushed myself up to a sitting position. "Grace?"

"I know you never liked the Tahoe, but still," Grace said. "I'm sorry."

I had no idea what she was talking about. I had inherited a white Tahoe SUV last summer but preferred my Jeep. I'd lent the Tahoe to Grace to use while they were in town.

"Tahoe?"

"Don't believe everything you hear. Tell Dad, 10-40." The call disconnected.

I was fully awake now. I knew what 10-40 was *supposed* to mean, but it didn't make any sense.

"Grace?"

I hit the callback button, but it went straight to voice mail. I clicked through my contacts and called Paul's phone. Voice mail.

"Mac, wake up." I shook his shoulder.

"I'm awake," he mumbled.

"Grace is in trouble."

Mac sat up slowly and clicked on the lamp by the bed.

"What?" He squinted at me in the newly bright room.

"That was Grace on the phone and she wasn't making sense." I punched redial and still got voice mail.

"What did she say?"

"Something about my Tahoe and a 10-code for Dad."

"Didn't you loan them the Tahoe while they were here?" Mac lay back down and reached for the light. "Maybe something happened to it."

"No, it sounded like something more than that." I swung my legs over the side of the bed and went to my closet to grab a pair of jeans and a sweatshirt. "I'm going over there."

"Now?" Mac also got out of bed, but he stood there as if still dazed from his rude awakening. His hair stood up in all directions. He reached for a T-shirt to pull on over his long flannel sleep pants.

"Yes, now." I yanked the hoodie over my head and pulled my hair into a ponytail. I grabbed my bag and walked into the hallway. It was so quiet here without Seth and the dogs.

"Wait, I'll come with you." He followed me into the hallway, tugging on jeans and trying to smooth his hair.

Mac and I climbed into my Jeep and drove the few blocks to my parent's house. The gravel driveway sent pinging rocks into the undercarriage and seemed very loud in the early morning stillness.

The house was dark and silent. As I stepped out of the car into the small clearing in front of the porch, it felt as if the house held its breath.

The Tahoe wasn't in the driveway.

I quietly mounted the steps and unlocked the door with the key that always sat over the doorframe. It swung open with a loud creak. Mac and I grimaced at each other and waited. I relaxed my shoulders, thinking we had gotten away with our sneaky entrance. And then the barking started. First, a low warning bark from Baxter, followed by a cacophony of high-pitched yips from Tuffy. At least that answered the question about their usefulness as guard dogs. Or at least intruder-alarm dogs.

A few moments after the noise began, Vi's door swung open, spilling light into the downstairs hallway. The upstairs light clicked on and Baxter barreled down the stairs, looking ferocious and annoyed. Tuffy scrabbled along the wood floor in his wake. They both skidded to a stop when they saw us and began their usual greeting dance.

"What's going on?" Vi said. She clutched a worn

purple robe at her neck, and her braid looked messy from sleep.

Seth and Sophie appeared on the upstairs landing, rubbing their eyes and yawning. Mom and Dad stood just behind them.

I walked over to Vi and in a low voice said, "Where's Grace?"

Vi glanced up the stairs to the landing. Then she walked to the foot of the stairs, her brow wrinkled.

"Rose, is Grace up there with you?"

Mom turned as if she expected Grace to be standing behind her. She hurried down the hall and we heard her click open the door to the guest room.

"Grace?" Mom's voice floated out of the room and down the stairs. I was getting more worried by the moment. Mac slid an arm over my shoulders.

"They're gone," Mom said when she returned to the landing.

"They said they were going to meet one of Grace's old high school friends in Grand Rapids tonight," Dad said.

"No, Frank," Mom said. "They're *gone*. Suitcases, clothing, everything."

Everyone spoke at once and I noticed Sophie leaning into Seth, looking scared.

"Let's sit down and figure this out," I said.

We all trooped into the living room. The kids sat on the floor, backs against the couch. Seth had his arm around Sophie and she stared at the adults with large eyes.

"Grace called me about a half hour ago to apologize

for the Tahoe and to say not to believe everything I hear," I turned to Dad. "She said to tell you, '10-40.'"

Dad frowned. "That means 'false alarm.'"

I leaned toward Dad. "That's what I thought. But it doesn't make sense. *What*'s a false alarm?"

Sophie whispered something to Seth. He turned to look at her and she nodded slowly.

"What is it, Sophie?" I asked.

She looked at each of us and seemed to sink further back into Seth.

"That's the code," she said.

"What code?" Vi said.

"She said she and Daddy might have to go away but they would be fine," Sophie said.

"You mean they were planning this?" I asked. "Seth, did you know about this?"

Seth shook his head.

Mac knelt down next to Sophie on the floor.

"Sophie, tell me exactly what your mom told you—it's very important," Mac said.

"She said that she would have to go away and that people might say she'd been in an accident, but it wasn't true." Sophie's eyes filled with tears. "She said that when it happened I probably wouldn't be able to see Miranda again."

"Who's Miranda?" Mom asked. "Come sit with me, sweetie. Tell us about Miranda."

Sophie got up and snuggled close to Mom on the couch.

"Miranda is my nanny. She takes care of me all the time. She takes me to school and makes my dinner and helps me with my homework. She goes to all my dance recitals and school things."

Mom looked at Vi and Dad and pulled Sophie closer.

"How long has she been taking care of you?" Mom asked. She pulled Sophie tighter and a long look passed between Mom and Dad.

"Since I was five," Sophie sniffled. "She always reads to me before I go to bed. Who will do that now?" Sophie's voice rose to a wail. I didn't think it was lost on any of us that Sophie was more concerned about her nanny than her possibly missing parents.

I was furious at Grace for doing this to her kids. Where did she think she was going and why would she have just left them like this?

Mac's phone rang and he pulled it out quickly to check who was calling at this hour of the morning. He clicked it open and stepped out of the room, his face blank except for the tight line of his mouth.

"I knew they were worried about something at work, but I had no idea it was this bad," Seth said.

Mac stepped back into the room and signaled for me to join him in the hallway. Mom took Sophie out to the kitchen to make hot cocoa for everyone. Dad looked shell-shocked, and for once Vi had nothing to say.

"That was the sheriff's office," Mac began. "They've found the Tahoe. He called because he wanted to give me some warning."

"Warning?"

"It's been found in Bailey Harbor at the marina. The lights were on and the alarm was sounding. They were able to trace the plate back to you."

"I don't understand," I said. "I thought they took the car and went somewhere."

He shook his head.

"The car was parked illegally on the dock. They must have driven through the barrier—the front end is smashed up and the fender is barely attached. The police got there in time to see a boat burst into flame out on the lake," Mac said. "The rip current was very strong today. They're searching for survivors, but they think anyone who jumped off the boat would be swept out into Lake Michigan." He reached out and pulled me closer. And through the roaring in my ears, I heard Seth gasp behind me.

21

❧

I turned quickly and saw Seth's stricken face. I stepped forward and hugged him. Even though he was taller than me, for those few moments I felt like he was a little kid again and I wished I could fix this as easily as I had fixed his broken toys back then.

Vi had followed Seth out into the hallway and she leaned against the wall, staring into space.

"I don't believe it," she said.

Mom called us back into the living room with demands to drink the cocoa while it was hot. She stopped fussing with the tray when she caught sight of our faces.

"What is it?" she said.

Mac cleared his throat. "There's been an accident."

Mom crumpled onto the couch next to Dad.

"When?" Dad asked. "Where?"

"In Bailey Harbor, earlier tonight. I'm waiting for the details." He waved his phone.

"Who was in an accident?" Sophie asked.

"They think it was Mom and Dad," Seth said. "The car they borrowed from Clyde was found . . ."

Sophie frowned and looked at each of us. "It isn't them."

Vi put her arm around Sophie. "I know it's hard to believe. But the car was definitely the one they were driving. It was found near a very bad boating accident."

Sophie began nodding even before Vi finished speaking. "I know that, but it isn't them."

"Sophie, I'm so sorry. It had to be them," I said. "It's definitely my car."

Sophie put her hands on her hips, just like my mom would do. "Mom said this would happen. She said you wouldn't believe it at first, but it isn't them."

"Wait, tell me about the accident your mom warned you about," I said.

Sophie nodded. "She said we would all have to pretend. She said I had the most important job. I had to tell you all that it isn't true."

I looked at Mac. He stepped back into the hall, his phone at his ear.

"I just don't know what to think," Mom said as the tears trailed quietly down her cheeks.

Seth looked like he might be sick and I was about to take him outside for some air when Mac came back in the room.

"Sophie might be right," he said. He smiled at her and she beamed adoringly at him.

"What?" Mom dabbed at her eyes and turned toward Mac.

"I just talked to the officer who responded to the call about the Tahoe," Mac said. "He said he was at the marina at two o'clock this morning."

"But I talked to Grace at three," I said.

"I knew it!" Vi said. "So they're okay?"

Mac held his hands out, palm up. "All I can say is if they were in the boat when it caught fire, they must have escaped. It was already demolished by the time Grace called."

"She told me not to believe everything I heard," I said.

"And a 10-40 is a false alarm," Dad said.

"But they're still gone," Mom said. "What do we do?"

I looked at Mac and we silently agreed that we wouldn't discuss Paul and Grace's concerns in front of the kids. However, they must have wanted it to look like they died in that boating accident.

"Kids, you might have to pretend a lot," I said. "Your parents were having some trouble at work and they hinted, although I didn't understand it at the time, that they might need to disappear for a while."

"What, like witness protection?" Seth asked. "I thought that was only for organized crime . . ."

I looked pointedly at Sophie and he stopped talking.

"They were worried about some bad men who were mad because they lost some money," Sophie said. "They blamed Mom and Dad, but it wasn't their fault."

"When did they tell you this?" Mac asked.

"Before we came here. They told me not to go with

anyone that wasn't a relative or Miranda." Sophie scowled. "Like I would just wander off with some stranger. That's when she told me that there would be an accident and we would have to pretend they had died. I can't even tell Miranda the truth."

Vi *hmph*ed and pulled Sophie closer. She looked at Mom over Sophie's head. Mom gripped her amethyst necklace, shook her head, and looked down at her lap.

"Sounds like Grace had it all figured out," Mac said dryly. "I just wish she would have warned us."

But I knew why she hadn't. She didn't want anyone to stop her.

22

Mom did what she always did in a crisis. She cooked. She dragged the kids to the kitchen to help make pancakes and bacon. Seth was an expert pancake flipper after months of tutoring from Alex. And Sophie knew how to microwave the bacon. Mom *tsk*ed at this newfangled technique, but it kept Sophie busy so she let her get on with it.

I made the coffee.

We gathered in the dining room just as the sky was beginning to lighten. After breakfast, both kids looked dazed and were yawning. I told Seth I would call his school and say he was staying home while we figured out what we were going to do. He and Sophie went back to bed, but I suspected they just wanted to be alone to talk.

The rest of us sat at the table to discuss the plan. I

told them about Grace's concerns and my suspicions that they had planned this to get out of trouble and to protect the kids. She must have decided they would be safer if their children couldn't be used as bargaining chips. If Grace and Paul were dead, there was no reason to come after the kids. I couldn't believe they would leave Seth and Sophie like that, but Grace had done a lot of things I couldn't believe.

"If they want everyone to think they're dead, then we're going to have to act as if they are," Vi said.

"We can do a memorial service for them here," Mom said.

"Do you think there will be an investigation into the boating accident?" Dad asked Mac.

"I don't know. Since the SUV has been identified and they're both missing, I think the authorities will assume they died in the fire. There wasn't much left of the boat.."

"But you said they haven't found any bodies," Mom said.

"That's true," Mac sipped his coffee. "The search and rescue will keep looking for a while, but with the rip current as strong as it is, they can't endanger the rescue crew, and they are already assuming they've drowned. It's unofficially turned from a rescue mission to a recovery mission. Grace and Paul likely staged the whole accident to make it look like they had died on the lake. They must have left the car with its alarm going off to attract attention and to be sure we got word right away. We don't know because they didn't tell us."

This was classic Grace. She trusted me with her

kids, but not with her plans to fake her own death. I wasn't sure how *I* would fake grieving at her memorial when I was so angry with her. Then I had another thought. And before I could voice it, Vi asked for me.

"You're sure it can't be true?" Vi's voice shook. "That they died in the fire or drowned?" She reached over and took Mom's hand in hers.

Mac leaned forward and spoke gently. "I talked to the officer myself. He was at the scene an hour before Grace called Clyde."

"Maybe he was paid off," I said. "Maybe this was the revenge they were so worried about."

Mac scooted his chair closer and draped an arm over my shoulders.

"That doesn't make sense," he said. "If the men that were after them had succeeded she wouldn't be able to call you."

"You're right," Dad said. "Grace had to be in on it, which means she's probably safe somewhere." Dad swirled his coffee cup, but didn't drink it.

"What are we going to do about Sophie?" I said to Mac.

Mac had just taken another swig of coffee. He swallowed wrong and choked.

"I hadn't even thought about that," he said. "If we have to tell the world that they're dead, then Rupert will expect us to take custody."

"That must be why she was so insistent that you sign the papers yesterday," Vi said. "I knew something was fishy about that—dragging Rupert over here on a weekend."

"I wonder why they suddenly had to rush things," I said. "Last week they said we could take our time deciding and by Sunday she was rushing it through. Do you think there was another threat?"

"Either that or there was another reason why they had to get out of town quickly," Mac said. He looked slowly around the table. "I hope the timing didn't have anything to do with Derek's murder."

Mom frowned. "What do you mean?"

"Yeah, what are you implying?" Vi crossed her arms and scowled. Which made me think she knew exactly what he was implying.

Mac held his hands out, palms up. "They were seen fighting with Derek. Grace has a history with Derek. Anyone would look into that connection."

Dad ran his hand through his hair. "Grace can be impulsive and selfish." He glanced at Mom and quickly continued. "She can even be dishonest and manipulative. But she's not a murderer."

"What about Paul?" I said. "Even after all the years they've been married, we hardly know him."

Mom gasped and grabbed her calming amulet. "How can you say that? Mac, you don't think one of them did it, do you?"

Mac held his hands up to stop the escalation. "I don't know what happened. And I'm not investigating anymore. I was taken off the case for this very reason."

"Will this Fisk person look into other suspects now?" Vi asked. "Or does the whole department think that just because Paul fought with Derek at the costume shop, he also killed him?"

There was a moment of silence as everyone processed what Vi had just said. Mac hadn't mentioned the costume shop. Vi knew about the fight.

"Vi, did you see the fight?" I asked.

Vi shrugged and looked at her lap.

Mac looked at me and then at Mom and Dad. "Detective Fisk will look at everyone again, I'm sure. But if he can't find another possibility, Grace and Paul will forever be suspect. Disappearing right now doesn't make them look innocent."

"Oh, my. What are we going to do?" Mom asked.

"Let's focus on Sophie and helping her get settled at our place," I said. "She can have the third bedroom." I turned toward my mother. "It's small, but you can help make it cozy for her."

"I'll take her shopping for things to decorate the room the way she wants," Mom said.

"I guess we should get her enrolled in school— maybe next week," I said.

I moved closer to Mac, and tried to calm my agitation.

We had just become a family.

23

It was only eight o'clock in the morning and I felt like I had already had a full and exhausting day. I recognized that the fewer people who knew the truth about Grace and Paul, the better. But I didn't see how I could keep it from Diana and Alex. Diana would figure it out just by looking at me, and Alex spent too much time with Seth not to realize that he wasn't truly grieving for his parents.

I texted them and asked them to meet us at Everyday Grill. Alex always closed on Monday mornings, but I knew he would be there organizing his supplies for the week and making menu changes.

Mac and I walked into town to clear the fog that had settled on our overtired brains. It was a beautiful spring morning. Birds made a racket in the trees, seemingly just as excited as the humans that warm weather was here to stay. The morning mist disappeared rapidly as the sun rose and warmed the ground. By the time we made it to the Grill, it had all burned off and the sun shone brilliant on the water in the marina.

The door was locked but Alex saw us and rushed to let us in. Diana was sitting at the table in the back, the one we always used for impromptu get-togethers like this one.

"You two look awful," she said when we slid into the chairs beside her.

Alex put two cups of coffee on the table and pushed mine toward me as if it was medicine and I was very ill.

"Is it Derek? Did you find out who did it?"

Mac shook his head.

"There's been an accident," I said. "Grace and Paul . . ." I stopped. How do you tell someone that your sister and her husband have faked their own death in order to escape the mob and possibly to avoid being arrested for murder?

Diana covered her mouth with a shaking hand and her eyes filled with tears. "Are they okay?"

I looked to Mac to help me tell this story.

"The car they were driving was found in Bailey Harbor near the marina. Just after it was found a boat caught fire on the lake." Mac held up his hand when Alex reached out to put his arm around me and Diana grabbed my hand. "We think they are unhurt."

"What does that mean, 'unhurt'?" Alex said. "Were they in the accident or not?"

"I got a call from Grace last night at three a.m.," I

said. "She was very cryptic and told me not to worry and that she was fine."

Mac said, "Later, I got a call from a friend in the department when they ran the plate on the car and discovered that it was Clyde's Tahoe."

"They stole your car?" Alex asked.

"So where are they?" Diana said.

"We don't know," I said. "Officially, they were in the boat when it burned, but the boat was found in flames at two a.m."

"An hour before you heard from Grace," Alex finished for me.

"I don't understand," Diana said.

"We don't really understand, either," I said. "Maybe I should back up." I told them the whole story: Grace's concern that they were in danger, her insistence that we sign the guardianship papers, Sophie's unshakeable belief that they were safe, and our conclusion that they want us to pretend they've been killed in order to protect the kids.

"Grace has really outdone herself this time," Diana said. Her mouth was pressed into a grim line. "I can't believe she would desert her kids like this. I mean, I know you always said she had minimal maternal instincts and it was only her skill at hiring good child care that kept the kids as happy as they've been, but this is going too far." Her voice rose in indignation.

"How *are* Seth and Sophie?" Alex asked.

"They seem okay so far," Mac said. "I'm not sure it's really sunk in yet what it means."

"Those poor kids," Diana said. She sniffed and

rubbed her eyes. She had lost her own parents about five years earlier. She'd been older than Seth and Sophie, and had already been living on her own, but it had still been devastating. She'd ended up taking care of her younger brother and dealing with all of the legal consequences.

"So this means you're their guardian?" Alex asked me.

I nodded. "And Mac. Grace insisted that we both sign the papers. I was irked at the time and thought she was trying to push us to . . . be more committed. Now I think she was planning this all along. Maybe she wanted Mac to buy in to the plan and not investigate the accident."

"What's next?" Alex asked. He leaned an elbow on the table and looked from me to Mac.

"We'll need to plan a funeral," I said. "Fortunately, Paul doesn't have any family so we don't need to lie to them. But if they want it to appear that they died in the car accident, we'll need to sell it."

Alex and Diana exchanged a look.

"What?" I said looking from one to the other.

"Well, it's just, you aren't the best liar," Diana said.

I wasn't sure if that was a compliment or an insult.

"I think I can attend a fake funeral and muster up some fake emotion." The fact that the emotion would be more anger than sadness hardly seemed to matter.

Diana tilted her head and pressed her lips together. Alex refused to meet my eyes.

"We'll work on it," Mac said. He smiled at me for the first time since Grace's early morning call.

* * *

Mac and I left Everyday Grill with Diana.

"Mac, I know you aren't working on the case anymore," Diana said. "But I asked Bethany about that ritual knife. She says it sounds like the one she sold to Tatiana. I told her you might want to talk to her."

That's where I remembered hearing about a knife. But how was Tatiana involved?

"Thank you, Diana." Mac gave her a warm smile. "I'll be sure the right person gets the information."

Diana turned left to head back to her shop, we turned right. I was about to ask Mac about the knife when I saw them—the same guys who had been following Grace and Paul the week before.

The zombie run and Founder's Day celebrations were over and most of the visitors had cleared out. What were *they* doing still in town?

"Mac . . ."

"I see them," Mac said quietly. "Just keep walking. Let's see what they do."

He took my hand and we strolled along the mainly empty sidewalk. Most of the businesses were closed on Mondays until June, or opened later in the morning. I had a prickly feeling on my neck as I turned my back on the men.

Mac walked with his head bent toward me as if we were talking intently. This allowed him to keep an eye on the men without letting them know we had noticed them.

"Are they following us?"

"They seem to be," Mac said. "They aren't very subtle about it. Maybe they're just walking in our general direction. If they're trying to be secretive, they're doing a terrible job."

"Maybe they *want* us to see them," I said. "Maybe it's a threat, not a botched tailing job."

"I suppose it's possible."

We turned right again to head back into our neighborhood. The men did not follow us and I was left wondering if I had imagined the whole thing.

24

❧

Later that day, the house buzzed with activity.
Mac and I had decided it would be best to move the kids
back to our house as soon as possible so they could get
used to their new home. Seth, of course, was already
used to it but now it was his *only* home.

Mom and Vi arrived with baskets of cleaning supplies, brooms, and rags as if I owned none of those
things. They bustled into the small third bedroom that
had been used as a dumping ground for out-of-season
clothing, shipping boxes needing to be recycled, and
anything else that didn't have a designated place in the
house. We all worked to clear it out and set it up com-
fortably for Sophie.

Dad arrived with his toolbox and disappeared into

the basement. The last time I had seen that toolbox, the fire department had been called. I had no idea what he planned to do down there, but gestured at Mac to go with him and supervise.

Mom unpacked Sophie's small suitcase and then took her to the mall to pick out bedding. I had the bed made up already, but the navy-blue-and-cream color scheme was deemed too sterile for a seven-year-old girl. The comforter they chose was definitely more colorful. The flowers and stripes represented every color of the rainbow.

The dogs were excited to be back in familiar surroundings and Tuffy got all of his toys out of the basket and left them in strategically inconvenient places around the house.

"Do you mind if we paint the room to go with the new bedding?" Mom said as she came downstairs into the living room.

I shook my head no and promptly stepped on one of Tuffy's hard chew toys. I swore under my breath and Tuffy came careening out of the kitchen to grab the toy. I sat and rubbed my foot, which Baxter took as an invitation to come over and drool on my shoulder.

Things were getting back to normal.

Tuesday morning we slept in after our mostly sleepless night on Sunday. Baxter had sensed Sophie's need for company and he lay outside her door, snoring, until she let him in. I found them curled up together the next morning—Sophie wedged between the dog and the wall while Baxter sprawled on her pillow.

Baxter opened one eye to check on the intruder and then closed it again in dismissal. I clicked the door shut quietly and followed the smell of coffee downstairs to the kitchen.

Mac sat at the table, his small notebook and multiple loose sheets of paper spread in front of him.

"What are you working on?" I asked as I poured a cup.

"I'm looking over my notes from the interviews," he said. He pointed to a pile on his left. "Derek's family. They all said he was a great guy without an enemy in the world."

I sat across from him.

He pointed to the next pile. "Witnesses from the zombie run. Before the run, Derek was seen talking to Grace, Tatiana, and his brother, Aaron. None of it looked friendly. But some people only saw a pirate zombie. So was it Paul talking to all these people or Derek?"

"I don't know why Paul would talk to Tatiana or Aaron. He didn't know either one of them."

"The zombie makeup doesn't help us," Mac said.

"Does Roy know about Grace's concerns about mistaken identity?"

"She and Paul mentioned it in their interviews, but they didn't give a good reason why anyone would want to hurt Paul. If I didn't know them, I would think it was an excuse to get the focus off of them as perpetrators and more as possible victims."

"I wish Grace and Paul had waited to hatch their disappearing plan," I said. I looked over the notes from his interview with Grace. "They aren't here now to defend themselves. A public brawl encourages gossip and there doesn't seem to be any other likely candidate."

"That's why I'm concerned." Mac tossed his pen onto the pile of papers. "If I didn't know Grace and Paul—and neither one of us really knew Paul—they would be my top suspects. Now that they have been 'killed,' it doesn't make things any better. They were told not to leave town and they snuck out in the middle of the night in an essentially stolen car . . ."

"I loaned them the Tahoe." I looked into my coffee mug to cover my own doubt about their motives in leaving the way they did.

"You're her sister. As an investigator, I'm going to assume now that she's dead, you're covering for her to keep her memory clean and pure for the children."

"So you'll try to get back on the case?"

Mac shook his head. "I'm now the guardian of the main suspects' kids. There's no way they'll let me anywhere near the case. My boss said I needed to stay away."

"Well, that's pretty clear then."

"Yes, it is." Mac smiled. "But that never stopped *you*."

We heard a door open upstairs and Mac quickly gathered his papers into a neat stack. Tuffy's nails scrabbled on the wood floor as he flew down the stairs and ran to the kitchen. Tuffy liked his breakfast immediately upon awakening.

Seth straggled after him and let the shih tzu out the back door to do his business. Seth smiled and mumbled good morning. Baxter ambled into the kitchen with Sophie and began wiggling happily when he saw Mac. Seth dumped dry food into the dog bowls and then showed Sophie our selection of cereals.

The kids brought their bowls to the table. Seth yawned and poured milk over the cereal in his bowl. Sophie picked at hers and ate it dry, like trail mix.

I got up and put some bread in the toaster.

"Sophie, do you want some toast?"

"Do you have peanut butter?"

"I think so." I rummaged in the cupboard and found a small jar. I showed it to her.

"Yes, please."

"Did you sleep okay in the new bed?"

She nodded. "Baxter took up most of it, but I liked having him with me."

"Nana Rose said she's going to have a memorial for Mom and Dad," Seth said in between bites of cereal. "It seems weird to have to act like they're dead. I don't understand why they had to go away."

I glanced at Mac and sighed. I resented needing to make up a story for the kids. I decided I just wouldn't. I could only protect them just so far and then they would need to know the truth.

"I don't really understand it, either," I said. "I know they got into some trouble in New York with some investors who lost a lot of money. These were people who could get pretty mean when things don't go their way."

"Mobsters," Sophie said. She had gotten up to spread peanut butter on her toast and I spun to look at her. She shrugged and licked her fingers. "We have Netflix."

"I'm sure if they saw any other way of keeping you safe, they would have done it," I said.

"I think the only other option would have been to take us with them, but that would have been hard." Seth said. "We'd have to go to school and this way they can keep moving if they need to."

Mac's eyebrows twitched upward. "What movies have *you* been watching? We might need to check the Netflix settings."

Seth smiled and went back to his focused eating.

"When do you want to go back to school, Seth?" I asked. "You can stay home this whole week if you want, but I don't want you to fall too far behind."

He lifted a shoulder. "I'll wait until Sophie starts."

"I have to go to school?" Sophie said.

"Of course you have to go to school," Seth said. "How are you ever going to get a job if you don't go to school?"

"I already know what I want to do and I just need Nana Rose and Aunt Vi to teach me."

"You still need to go to school, Sophie." I said. "You might change your mind and besides, it's against the law to not go to school."

"Oh, right." She finished off her toast and sat for a moment, chewing. "Will all the kids know that we're orphans?"

Oh boy. I'd seriously have to get a handle on the movie watching.

"I'm not sure if they will or not. They might, especially since we're going to have a memorial service. We need to do that so that the people who were after your parents will believe that they died in the accident."

She sighed. "Okay."

25

"I just want to get this over with," Mom said that afternoon. She had papers and lists strewn on the table in front of her.

"We have to make it believable, Rose," Vi said. "Grace is counting on us."

"I would have thought that if she needed our help so desperately, she could have told us what she was planning," Mom grumbled. "I will *never* forgive her for putting us through that the other night. I thought she was dead."

Vi patted Mom's hand and made soothing noises. The list of things Grace would never be forgiven for had grown quite long. I almost didn't blame her for wanting to start over somewhere new.

"I already talked to Reverend Frew," I said. "He says

we can do the memorial tomorrow afternoon. Will that be enough time to notify everyone?"

Mom nodded.

Vi pulled the list of mourners toward her side of the table. "We have most of these people on standby already. It will be very small. I'm glad there's no one from out of town on the list. We can put this all behind us by tomorrow evening."

Except for the fact that I was now in charge of two kids for the foreseeable future. A year ago, I was single, living in Ann Arbor, and working my way up the ladder at the police department. Now I was in a relationship, unemployed, with two kids to raise. My head spun as I contemplated it all.

Dad had taken the kids to a movie so we could focus on making plans for the memorial service. I hoped we would be able to pull this off. Keeping it small was a great idea; fewer people to notice if we were not acting as if someone had died.

"Alex said he would take care of the food and everyone can go to the restaurant after the service," I said.

Mom made a note on one of her pieces of paper.

"I wonder where they are now," Vi said.

Mom glanced at Vi and then away. She brushed tears off her cheek and took a deep breath. "I just hope they're safe."

"We have to assume that they are," I said. "They're both very clever. And . . . the men that were following them are still in town. I saw them earlier."

"What? Do you think they're after you now, or the kids?" Mom's hands fluttered from her chest to her mouth.

"I don't know, but I don't see why they would be."
I hesitated. "They could be watching all of us. Maybe
they suspect the accident was a fake and they want to
see how we act."

"We'll play it up." Vi said. "We'll throw a big memorial and look sad whenever we're out in town."

"I've already talked to the kids and they're on board.
I think getting the memorial over with as soon as possible will be good and maybe the men will move on."

The organ droned out a melancholy march the next
afternoon as the mourners filed in. There was a good
turnout considering Grace hadn't been seen in town
in fifteen years. Mom had overordered on the flowers
and the mixture of the scents was so strong, the air felt
thick with it.

I sat in the front pew with Seth, Sophie, and Mac.
Mom, Dad, and Vi were across the aisle.

The kids had been coached again on their need to
act somber.

I pretended to whisper something to Mac so I could
scan the pews behind us. I was watching for the two
stalkers. I had asked Diana to stay at the back and keep
her eye out as well. Alex was already at the restaurant
preparing for the reception.

Reverend Frew slowly mounted the steps onto the
pulpit and cleared his throat.

"We are gathered today to mark the passing of
Grace Fortune Proffit and her husband, Paul Proffit.
Two lives cut short by chance and circumstance . . ."

I tuned him out. I had been to plenty of funerals since I returned to Crystal Haven less than a year ago, and listening to a fake eulogy seemed wrong somehow. Plus, listening to all of Grace's wonderful attributes while I was carrying a justifiable grudge would only serve to irritate.

I saw Mom dab at her eyes although I could see she wasn't crying. Vi put her arm over Mom's shoulder. The two of them had practiced this at home, making sure it appeared from behind that they were distraught. Dad sighed and stole a glance at his watch, which earned a jab in the ribs from Mom. I wondered how *that* had played to the back row.

Jillian and Tom sat a few rows behind Mom and I could see that Jillian was truly crying. Tom had tried to offer condolences yesterday when I saw him in town and he'd been unable to get through it without his voice cracking and his nose turning red.

All of this only fueled my anger at my sister. What did she care that we had to lie to people we cared about and that they would feel helpless in the face of our perceived loss? Why did she have to come all the way here to have her fake accident?

I stood with relief when the strains of *Amazing Grace* boomed out of the organ—our cue that the family could progress out of the church.

The day was bright with a painfully clear blue sky. Tulips dotted the walkway out of the church and the grass was that bright spring green of late April. We milled about for a few minutes and then arranged ourselves in a line to greet the guests. I had explained this part to the kids and told them they didn't have to stand in the line, but they both insisted it would look weird and that they could handle it.

And they did. Appropriately solemn, but not overdone, Seth and Sophie shook hands and accepted condolences. Vi, on the other hand, cried loudly and messily next to Mom, who stood as if in a trance with the slightest smile on her face. I nudged her to get her attention.

"You're smiling, quit it."

She pulled her face into a mask of sadness. "I have something to tell you after this is over," she whispered and turned to the next person in line.

26

∾∾

Everyday Grill was packed when we arrived.
Memorial aside, people always turned out for free food.

We had dropped the kids off at home to watch a
movie. I didn't want to subject them to any more comments from well-meaning strangers.

I hesitated in the doorway and took a deep breath.
Mac squeezed my hand reassuringly and pulled me into
the room.

"There you are!" Vi hurried to my side. "This is a
pretty good turnout for Grace and Paul. I think it's
mostly because everyone just loves your mother."

A plate of food was pushed into my hands and I
picked at it while nodding and thanking people for
coming. I felt like such a fraud. Some of Grace's high
school friends approached; they clutched wineglasses

and sniffled. It seems the memorial had triggered them to reconsider their bucket list. There was a lot of talk about what they will do with the short time they have. Even though they were barely forty years old, they acted like they were all at death's door.

After listening to a few stories about Grace's high school exploits, I took Mac's hand and pulled him off to the side. I needed a break from the grief of other people, grief I obviously didn't share. We snuck behind a large potted plant and I leaned against him.

"Are you doing okay?" his voice was low and quiet.

I nodded and looked up at him.

A familiar voice spoke from the other side of the plant. "I heard Derek was flirting with her and the husband got so angry he swung at Derek without any warning."

Harriet Munson. Great. The whole town would think Grace was a murderer by the end of her memorial.

"No, I heard it was Derek that started it." This sounded like Tatiana and I pulled a few leaves aside to peek. Harriet, Tatiana, and Theo stood about five feet away, their backs to our hiding place. "He walked right up to them and started insulting the husband. They said he acted like he was drunk."

"Derek was always volatile," Theo said. "Not like his brother. Aaron is as calm as they come."

"What a shame," Tatiana said. "Can you believe they died within a couple of days of each other?"

The gossipers moved away and I couldn't hear anymore. Mac held me tighter and we waited a couple of minutes before appearing again in the room.

As if the mention of his name had caused his

appearance, Aaron Vaughn wended his way through the crowd toward us.

"Hello, Clyde, Mac," he said. He put out his hand to us both. "Clyde, I'm so sorry for your loss. Grace was very special."

"Thank you," I said.

"I wonder if I might have a word with you?" He looked at me and tilted his head toward the door.

I glanced at Mac and gave him a brief nod. "Sure."

Aaron led the way out onto the sidewalk.

"What can I do for you, Aaron?" I asked. Had he heard people talking about the fight? Surely he didn't think Grace or Paul had killed his brother? I crossed my arms to ward off a chill that had nothing to do with the weather.

"My son, Logan, works at the animal shelter with Seth," he said.

I nodded. Maybe Seth had told Logan about the fight? Did Seth even know about the fight? I couldn't remember anymore who knew what.

"He tells me that you and your aunt have started a business together."

I uncrossed my arms. This was a surprise.

"Yes, we have."

"I'd like to hire you." He glanced up and down the street and lowered his voice even though we were quite alone. "I need to be sure that this will be in strict confidence. "

"You know what kind of a business we have? I have a PI license but I don't do divorce work or collections." We'd had a couple of inquiries where the *finding* aspect of our business had been misinterpreted. They thought we could find a husband's mistress or a person who owed money.

He held up his hands. "I assure you I know exactly what you do and I need you to find something for me."

A couple of people came through the door of the restaurant and stopped when they saw Aaron and me standing on the sidewalk. I saw the exchanged glance and gleam of newly acquired gossip.

"Maybe we should discuss this privately," I said.

His face relaxed and he smiled. "I would appreciate that."

"Come by my house this afternoon. Around four."

He nodded and I left him standing outside on the sidewalk.

I reentered the restaurant and blinked a few times after the brightness of the day.

"There you are!" Vi said. She grabbed my hand and pulled me toward the back of the restaurant. "Your father and Richard Vaughn are brawling in the back."

"What?" I followed quickly and pulled my hand away when we got to the kitchen door.

We peeked through the glass window.

I couldn't believe what I was seeing. Dad and Richard had each other in a headlock and their "brawl" consisted of grunting and turning in a circle as each man tried to get a better grip. Vi pushed the door open and we slipped inside. The combatants muttered to each other, but I couldn't make out what they were saying. Mom stood to one side, wringing her hands and looking mortified. I looked around for Richard's wife, but she wasn't there. I didn't remember seeing her at the memorial. Maybe she hadn't been there. The kitchen staff stood transfixed and Vi watched with undisguised glee.

When the large bowl of salad clattered to the floor, covering the entire kitchen in green, Vi grabbed a large bucket of melting ice and water and tossed it onto the two men. They pulled apart, dripping and angry and turned on Vi.

She shrugged and set the bucket down. "It works with dogs and cats, too."

Mac and Alex stepped in while the fighters were still stunned from the ice water.

Mac pulled Richard's arms behind him but seemed to be struggling to keep control. Alex faced Dad, keeping himself between the two pugilists. Dad's face was red and his hair was askew, making him look like an angry cockatoo.

Shards of plates lay smashed next to the main prep table, and oil dripped onto them from a bottle of olive oil that had been knocked over. Salad draped and dripped everywhere and large metal bowls sat upended on the floor. I saw one of the kitchen staff pull a large butcher's knife off the counter and quietly slide it into a drawer.

"What is going on here?" I said. I put my hands on my hips and adopted my angry cop stance. Where was Charla when I needed her?

"Mom, why don't you take Dad outside to cool off?" I gestured toward the door that led into the back alley.

"Mr. Vaughn, your son is out front," I said. "I suggest you go now."

Richard Vaughn cast a menacing glance at Dad's back, shrugged Mac off, and strode out of the kitchen.

"Alex, what happened?" I said. "I'll help you clean up."

The door swung open and Diana and Lucan came through.

"What's going on?" Diana asked. "We just saw Richard Vaughn storm out the front door." She lowered her voice. "He was soaking wet and I think he had salad in his hair."

I closed my eyes slowly and took a deep breath.

"You wouldn't believe it," Vi said. "Richard said something to Frank about Grace leaving Derek all those years ago. And your father said she was better off. And then Richard said, 'Like Rose? I'm sure she's had time over the years to regret her choice,' and then your father attacked him."

"Dad? Attacked Richard?" I said.

"Well, he told him to step into the kitchen, and *then* he attacked him."

Alex was shaking his head. "That's not what happened."

Vi crossed her arms and narrowed her eyes at Alex.

"They came through the door, arguing," Alex said. "Richard was in front and Frank was right behind him—they were definitely angry. Then one of the servers came through the door right behind them and the door slammed into Frank, who stumbled forward and pushed Richard. Richard turned and took a swing at Frank and then we had to pull them apart."

Mac nodded. "I didn't see the beginning, but I saw

them arguing and followed them into the kitchen. They were already swinging away when I got here."

"They took out the whole counter of salad," Vi said and pointed to the mess on the floor.

Mac chuckled. Then Alex started to laugh. Pretty soon we were all laughing at the idea of my dad and Richard Vaughn wrestling in a pile of salad.

Harriet Munson peeked through the door with an angry scowl. "Really, Violet, I would expect a bit more decorum at a time like this."

We quickly sobered up and looked contritely at Harriet. Diana and Lucan slid past her and back out into the restaurant.

Mac and I began to pick up the mess, but Alex shooed us out of the kitchen.

The crowd grew quiet as we stepped back through the door. All eyes watching.

"There's been a small accident in the kitchen," Mac said. "We'll have to skip the salad and go straight to dessert."

27

I pulled the door wide to allow Aaron and Richard Vaughn and Theo Lancaster to enter. I was surprised Aaron hadn't come alone. I'd gotten the impression he wanted to keep the whole thing a secret. It felt weird to be in the same room with Richard Vaughn now that I knew about his history with my mother. I couldn't imagine Mom with anyone but Dad, and this man had almost married her. I could see why she had been attracted to him. Even now, he was a good-looking man, though currently marred by a puffy right eye—go Dad. He was tall, with silver hair and bright, intelligent eyes.

"Thank you for seeing us," he said. "I know this has been a difficult week for you. I knew your sister when she was younger and she was a charming girl."

"Thank you, and I'm sorry for your loss as well. Please, have a seat." I gestured toward the living room. "Can I get you anything?"

Theo took the armchair. Richard and Aaron sat on the couch and leaned forward, elbows on knees, in identical postures. "No, thank you," Richard said. "I'll get right to the point. We'd like to hire you for a rather delicate situation."

I nodded that he should continue.

"We're . . . missing a large portion of our inventory and we'd like you to find it."

"Inventory? What kind of inventory?"

"Diamonds," Aaron said. "Thirty diamonds, all between one and three carats, went missing from our safe last week."

"Don't you think this is a matter for the police?" I asked. "If you were burgled . . ."

Richard shook his head and held his hand up. "We don't want to involve the police."

"I'm not sure what you think I can do," I said. "I don't really handle this sort of thing. I can find items, certainly, but I don't track down stolen goods."

Aaron pressed his lips together and hesitated for a moment.

"We know who took the diamonds. We just don't know what he did with them and we'd really like to recover our property."

"I don't understand," I said. "If you know who took them, it should be very easy for the police to find this person and compel him to turn over the jewels."

"It was Derek who took the diamonds," Richard

said. He rubbed his face and then stopped suddenly when he touched his swollen eye.

I took a quick breath. I hadn't expected this. "Perfect" Derek had stolen from his family's jewelry store?

"Are you sure about this?"

"We have it on video." Aaron clasped his hands loosely between his knees. "We have seen all of the personal effects that were found by the police, which means he must have hidden them before he was killed."

"Maybe whoever killed him stole the diamonds," I said. "There have been worse motives."

"We thought of that," Theo began, "but have reason to believe that Derek stole the diamonds to pay off a debt. Those people wouldn't have killed him if he'd given them the diamonds."

"Maybe it was someone else," I said. "Who else might have known about the missing diamonds?"

A glance passed between Aaron and Theo.

"We're the only people who know any diamonds are missing," Richard said.

"Unless his killer accidently discovered the jewels after he was dead, we don't think his killer took them," Aaron said.

"I know this is a difficult time for you," Richard said, "but with Grace and Paul's flight from town, doesn't it seem likely that they were involved?"

"Dad!" Aaron said. He glowered at his father. Theo looked embarrassed and studied the carpet.

I inhaled quickly and prepared to defend Grace and Paul when I remembered that I had no proof they didn't do it, and no other likely suspect.

I sat up straight and shook my head. "There is nothing linking them to Derek's murder." I heard the steely tone creep into my voice. I liked Richard Vaughn less and less. I found myself wishing Dad had a better right hook.

"We don't want to get into an argument about Grace's guilt or innocence," Theo said. He held his hands out in a placating gesture. "*I* don't think she had anything to do with it. We were hoping you could simply help us find the diamonds. Even a general idea of their location would be useful."

I stood and went to the window to look out at the sunny spring afternoon. My radar was ringing and I didn't trust Richard, but one way to find out more about this family and maybe help solve the murder was to agree to help them.

"Okay," I said. "I'll see what I can do."

"What's your fee?" Richard stood to pull out his wallet.

Vi said we should always charge ten percent of the worth of the item. That got a little tricky when the item was worthless to anyone but the owner. Knowing it was diamonds he was looking for, I didn't think I could charge him ten percent. If my methods worked, it only took a few minutes.

"Five percent of the worth of the recovered items."

His smile slipped into a smirk and I regretted giving him a break. "Done. In fact, if you deliver them within the week and keep this between us, I'll give you six percent."

Again I felt that frisson of warning, but I put my hand out to shake on the deal.

"I'll be in touch as soon as I have some news for you." I walked to the door, anxious to end this conversation.

"How long does it usually take?" Aaron asked.

"It depends, but at least a couple of days."

Richard nodded and pulled five hundred-dollar bills out of his wallet. He held them out to me. "I assume you require a retainer?"

Since most of my clients so far had been owners of lost cats, I'd never received a retainer. I pocketed the money and thought anxiously about the lecture I would receive from Vi when she found out about my discount deal.

"I'd appreciate it if you would give this your undivided attention," Richard said as I opened the front door.

"Of course, top of the list," I said.

"I'm very sorry for your loss," Aaron said. "Grace was . . . one of a kind."

"Some of my best memories are times I spent with your sister," Theo said. "I'm very sorry."

I closed the door behind them and leaned against it. I let out a long breath and waited for the irritation to subside.

I went to the kitchen to make tea and think.

Mac had taken the kids and the dogs out for a walk in the woods. I'd told them to stay away until about five o'clock. I was glad for the time to myself.

Derek had stolen diamonds from his family's business. Why? I remembered the rumors that he had been a gambler. I supposed he could have debts from that. The whole story was strange. He must have known about the security cameras. Unless he didn't know they were there?

If I were investigating the crime, that's something I would want to know, but I wasn't. I was only hired to *find* the diamonds, not analyze why he had taken them.

I was too hyped up from the memorial, the brawl, and this new news to focus on finding the diamonds.

The electric kettle clicked off and I poured the water into a mug.

Besides finding stolen diamonds, trying to keep my sister and her husband from being accused of murder, and keeping my father out of any more brawls, I would have to get Sophie signed up for school and figure out how to get all of her stuff shipped here from New York.

I sat at the table with my tea and pulled a blank piece of paper off the top of Mac's pile of papers. I would need a list to keep track of everything. I'd also need to contact Rupert and find out what else the will contained besides giving me custody of the kids. At least I could accomplish that much. I reached for the phone and dialed.

I took a sip of tea. How did my life turn upside down so quickly?

28

My head was still spinning from my conversation with Rupert when the dogs, the kids, and Mac burst in the door. They brought the damp smell of earth, leaves, and fresh spring air in with them.

Tuffy and Baxter made a beeline for the kitchen and both sat in front of their dinner bowls. Seth had taught them this trick and it was so much better than the nudging, whining, and pathetic stares that had been their previous method of asking for dinner.

Seth followed them in with Sophie right behind. She had been more closely attached to Seth than his shadow since Grace and Paul had disappeared, and I marveled again that Seth tolerated it with such good humor. I thought that his empathy for animals might extend to certain humans as well.

"There you are," Seth said to me. "Is Logan's dad gone? What did he want?" Seth swung open the refrigerator and pulled out the dog food.

Sophie bent and picked up the bowls, which caused Baxter to lie down quietly, and Tuffy to begin leaping into the air. Seth had not been able to convince him that his acrobatics were not actually helpful and would not speed up the delivery of food.

"He wanted to hire me and Vi to find something," I said, and avoided meeting his gaze.

"Is it Draco?" he asked.

I looked at him blankly.

"Logan's pet snake," Seth rolled his eyes at me as if I should know who Draco was. He spooned the food into the bowls.

"No, it's not a missing pet case," I said.

"Oh, good," Seth said. "Logan's pretty attached to that thing and his mother keeps threatening to set it free in the woods."

Another thing I'd rather not know.

"As far as I know, Draco the snake is safe at home."

"So what did he want?" Seth handed a bowl to Sophie for Baxter and put Tuffy's bowl on the floor.

"Who?" Were we still talking about the snake?

"Logan's dad," Seth said. He was bent over Tuffy, fixing his collar while the little dog inhaled his food. "What did he want?"

"He asked me not to talk about it," I said.

Seth stood and crossed his arms. "Everything's a secret with them."

"What do you mean?"

Seth shrugged. "Logan says his grandfather has a terrible temper and they can't ever tell him anything."

"Is that all?"

Seth glanced at Sophie and then back at me. "Well, he says ever since the events at the zombie run his parents have been whispering to each other all the time and acting weird. He said his mom was crying when he came home from school and she never cries."

"Well, the family is going through a really tough time right now," I said. "I'm sure things will calm down when the police are finished with their investigation."

"He says the only person acting normal is Theo," Seth said.

"Does he spend a lot of time with Theo Lancaster?" I asked.

Seth shrugged. "I guess. He says Theo is more like an uncle than Derek ever was."

"Hmm. I got that impression as well."

Sophie had been watching our exchange and she jumped in as soon as there was a lull. "I'm hungry, Aunt Clyde."

"What do you guys want for dinner?"

"Mac says we can have pizza," Sophie said. "I like pineapple, but Seth likes mushrooms." She made a disgusted face.

"We can get both, I said." Based on what Rupert had told me, they could buy the whole store. "Why don't you and Seth go pick a movie to watch and I'll order the pizza?"

Sophie skipped into the living room, dragging Seth behind her.

"No princesses or unicorns," Seth grumbled.

"Okay," Sophie said.

"Pick something funny," I said. "No scary movies."

I heard the television click on, and the kids began discussing choices.

Mac walked into the kitchen and both dogs wagged their tails while continuing to eat. I wanted to tell Mac about the Vaughns' story of the diamonds, and struggled with my promise to keep it a secret. If Mac could get word to Roy that Derek had stolen diamonds from his family, it would give them another area of inquiry into his death. Either way, I didn't want to talk about it now, when there was a chance of being interrupted by the kids.

"So, pizza?" I said.

Mac grinned. He and Seth loved pizza and would have it almost every night. With Sophie living here, I would have one more vote against me in the great pizza debate.

Mac put his arms around me and rested his head on top of mine.

"I'll let you pick the toppings," he said.

"Only because you know I like the same ones you do."

"You do?" He pulled away and looked down into my face. "How lucky is that?"

I grinned and pushed him away. "You order. Sophie wants pineapple, and she doesn't want any of Seth's mushrooms touching her half."

Mac clicked open his phone and dialed.

* * *

Later that night, Mac and I picked up the pizza boxes, plates, and napkins from the living room coffee table while Baxter and Tuffy examined the carpet for any stray pieces of cheese or pepperoni. Seth had agreed to read the Lemony Snicket books to Sophie and I could hear his voice floating down from the top of the stairs as he told the sad tale of the Baudelaire orphans. It occurred to me that they should have picked a series that didn't involve orphans and evil guardians, but it was too late.

Mac clipped on the dogs' leashes.

I went to the bottom of the stairs and called up. "Kids! We're taking the dogs out. We'll be right back."

Seth stopped reading. "Okay."

Tuffy glowered up the stairs and sat. He hated it when anyone other than Seth took him for a walk. Baxter wagged his whole body and weaved in and out between Mac and me. Tuffy finally gave in and allowed me to pull him out the door.

The cool night air made both dogs happy and they sniffed along the sidewalk like they were reading a good book.

I decided to take advantage of our five minutes alone to tell Mac my news from Rupert.

"I spoke to Rupert earlier this evening," I said. "He told me about the money Grace and Paul left in trust for the kids."

Mac stopped and turned to me. Baxter tugged for a moment at the leash and then sat with a dramatic sigh.

"I got the impression that they didn't have any money after all the troubles with the Milano family."

I shrugged. "I don't know how they did it, but they have an account for the kids. It's for their college and health insurance and maybe a yacht . . ."

"What?"

I told him the amount in the bank account.

He blinked. He didn't say anything. We walked in silence for a few moments.

"I'm . . . I don't know what to say."

I nodded. That was pretty much my reaction when Rupert told me.

"I guess I can stop worrying about how we'll support them," Mac said.

"Rupert has been named the executor, so he will oversee the accounts, but they also arranged for a very generous monthly stipend."

"Is this what you've been thinking about all evening?" Mac asked.

"What?"

"You've been in a different world since the Vaughns visited." Mac turned to look at me. "I thought it had to do with them, I knew something was bothering you."

I bent to pet Baxter and avoided Mac's eyes. I didn't know what to do. I had made a promise to the Vaughns and Theo to keep their request a secret, but something about it didn't feel right. On the other hand, Mac wasn't actually working this case.

I stood and smiled. "I was a bit thrown by the amount of money. And after the chaos this afternoon, the whole guardianship thing is starting to sink in." I pulled on Tuffy's leash to keep him from digging in Mrs. Munson's flowers. He was very attracted to her tulips.

Mac seemed satisfied with this partial truth and I resolved to find the diamonds and figure out if I needed to involve the police.

That night, after the kids had gone to bed and Mac had fallen asleep quickly and deeply, I slid out of bed and tiptoed downstairs. I needed quiet to concentrate and it was obvious to me that quiet was going to be in short supply from now on.

I took the blanket off the back of the couch and wrapped it around my shoulders as I made myself comfortable on the couch. Bright silver light from the full moon and the dim streetlights cast everything in a bluish glow. I took a deep breath and let it out slowly. I closed my eyes and concentrated on the diamonds.

At first nothing came to me. My own thoughts intruded. I worried about Grace and Paul and where they might be and whether they were in danger. How would we know if they were being followed, or had been found by whoever was after them? I worried it would be a very long time before they could return. Maybe they never would. How would this affect the kids? They seemed fine right now because it was all new and might even feel like a vacation, but once Sophie started school and realized she had to stay here, how would she feel then? How would she adjust to life without Miranda, who was arguably more of a caregiver than Grace had ever been?

I opened my eyes. I had to try again. Three slow, deep breaths this time. I focused on the diamonds and whenever a stray thought about the kids or my sister threatened to intrude, I pushed it gently aside to deal with later. The goal was to completely empty my mind so that I could be receptive to the location of the diamonds. Neila and I had worked on this technique in the past couple of months since I had given in to Vi's insistence that we open a business together. In the past, I had approached this part of my talent in a haphazard fashion. If a location came, fine. If not, I'd just wait and see.

Now that I was getting paid, I had to be more regimented and Neila had helped me to develop a system that usually worked. I had found several lost pets and belongings since we started taking clients.

My mind was blank and I focused only on my breathing. In and out. Then I felt it. It was just a tiny tug, but I knew I had been given a hint. Only it didn't make sense. I felt a tug toward the animal shelter. I must have begun thinking about Seth and the zombie run.

I tried again. Still, the animal shelter showed up, more clearly this time. I tried to move my mind away from the shelter and push it in a different direction. I thought about Derek in the woods but my brain kept coming back to the shelter. It felt a bit like a game of hot and cold. I could imagine locations and get a feel for whether it was a likely place to look. Every reasonable place I thought of felt cold and the shelter felt hot.

After another few minutes of trying to convince

myself that I was wrong, I had to give up. I climbed the stairs quietly and slipped into bed next to Mac. How was I going to search the animal shelter without raising suspicion? It was more likely I would find a lost pet than stolen diamonds.

29

❦

Thursday morning, Seth and Sophie bounded out of the Jeep and chattered all the way in to the animal shelter. Sophie wanted to check on the bunnies that had been dropped off after Easter and Seth had heard from Logan that there was a Great Dane that had been brought in after its owners decided to move back to the city. There was only one other car in the parking lot.

I followed more slowly, trying to tap into whatever I had sensed the night before. I still felt that tug toward the building even though I couldn't fathom any reason why the diamonds would be at the animal shelter. I had found in recent months while working with Neila, and after taking on a few clients, that I had to quiet my rational mind and allow the feelings to take center stage. Not an easy task for a person who had been trained to focus on concrete facts. But if the lost item were anywhere rational, it wouldn't be lost, would it?

I pushed open the door and stepped inside. Fortunately, the lobby was empty. Standing in the middle of the room, arms loose at my sides, I took deep slow breaths. The key was to remain relaxed. If I forced it, or tried to impose my ideas of where an item might be, I would never get a clear picture.

I heard Seth and Sophie moving along the cages on the other side of the swinging door. Francine spoke to them, giving Seth a list of jobs and telling Sophie about the bunnies. Dogs barked and whined as they moved toward the back of the shelter. I was definitely sensing that the diamonds were not behind that door.

My mind began to focus on the break room behind the front desk. There was a short hall to the left of the reception area that housed the small office, an exam room, some storage, and a tiny room where volunteers kept spare clothing and left their belongings when they came to work. That is where I felt I should go.

I scooted around the reception desk and hurried down the hall. Scanning the room from the doorway, I noted a small fridge and microwave nestled in the corner by the sink. A battered table and folding chairs took up most of the space in the middle of the room. Along the right-side wall, a row of cubbies spilled clothing, leashes, paper towels, and bedding. I walked toward it and waited.

Lower left. My mind focused on that corner of the unit. I knelt and pulled out an old gray sweatshirt, a pair of green scrub pants, and a pack of gum. At the very back of the cubby in the corner I felt a velvet pouch.

I could hardly believe it. Every time I found something using this method I was amazed. I clutched the bag and drew it out. My hand shook as I loosened the drawstring. I dumped the contents into my palm. A pile of sparkling stones fell out.

"What are you doing?" Francine said.

I startled and almost dropped the jewels. I closed my fist and stood. I had dropped the bag, and I shoved it under the shelf with the toe of my shoe. Next to Jillian Andrews, Francine was the main source of gossip in town. If she thought I was looking for something, everyone would know before I even got back home.

"I was just looking for Seth's cubby," I lied. "He said he got his things muddy last week and of course he didn't think to bring them home."

"Seth's stuff is here." Francine came forward and pulled clothing out of a top cubby at the other end of the storage unit.

"Oh, this looked like his sweatshirt." I held up the hoodie while shoving the diamonds into my pants pocket.

Francine nodded. "That's Logan's stuff. They're about the same size."

I pushed the scrubs and sweatshirt back into the cubby and took the old jeans and T-shirt that Francine held out.

"How are the kids doing?" she asked. "They seem fine, but you can never tell with kids."

"I think they're okay," I said. "It's a big adjustment, and I'm not sure it's really sunk in yet."

My palms felt damp, and I could feel my heart pounding in my chest. I wanted to get out of there and examine the stones. Aaron said there were thirty of them. I couldn't tell if I had found the whole stash or if whoever had hidden them had split them up.

"Seth's a good kid," Francine said. "He's a hard worker and he seems to really understand the animals and what they need."

I smiled. She had no idea how well Seth understood. "Thanks, I'm glad it's working out. He likes coming here."

"It's hard to believe we had two tragedies so close together," Francine said. She leaned against the table and crossed her arms.

I nodded and pretended to examine Seth's sweatshirt for mud.

"I feel terrible for Logan, but I wish people would stop blaming your sister. She's not the only one with a link to Derek."

I looked up at her but she was staring out the window at the dogs in the fenced pen.

I cleared my throat. "What do you mean she's not the only one?"

I caught the glimmer in Francine's eyes as she looked back at me. It was the same look Jillian got when she found someone who hadn't heard her "news" yet.

"Lila and Derek. Aaron's wife?" She leaned closer and lowered her voice. "After your sister left town, he took up with Lila for a while."

"What?" I glanced at the door. I didn't want the kids to overhear this. I whispered, "Did Aaron know?"

Francine shrugged. "Lila and I were good friends in high school. After the thing with Derek, she pulled away from everyone here and set up her new life in Grand Rapids." She pushed away from the table and went to the door. "He probably doesn't know. If he did, Derek would have been dead a lot earlier than this."

Twenty minutes later, I nervously pulled onto Singapore Highway from the shelter parking lot, acutely aware of the tens of thousands worth of diamonds in my pocket.

Seth and Sophie chatted loudly over the music and it took a moment for me to realize Sophie was asking me a question.

"So can we?"

"Can we what?" I asked, concerned I had missed something important.

"Adopt a kitten."

My shoulders slumped. I didn't want to disappoint Sophie, but I didn't think a cat would fit in with Tuffy and Baxter.

"I don't know, Sophie." I turned in my seat to look back at her. Out of the corner of my eye, I saw a black sedan parked along the road, tucked in the trees. It pulled onto the road behind us as we passed. I glanced in my rearview and saw that it stayed well back from my Jeep. But I had seen the driver. It was Flattop.

Why were they following us?

I thought that with Grace and Paul "dead," they

would have gone back to wherever they came from. Could they be following the kids? Had Grace and Paul's plan failed?

"What's going on?" Sophie asked.

Singapore Highway twisted through the trees and I stepped on the gas just to see what the other car would do. It sped up as well. Seth turned to look behind us. He shushed Sophie and she twisted in her seat as well.

"Hey, it's the watchers!" she said. "Why are they following us?"

"I'm not sure, Soph." I said.

We were about two miles outside of Crystal Haven. I slowed back to the speed limit. They weren't actively threatening, but it seemed like they had been waiting for us.

"Should we go to the police station?" Seth asked.

"Police?" Sophie squeaked. "Are they going to hurt us?"

"No," I said. "They aren't going to do anything. That's a good idea, Seth."

I took the right fork that led into town and then turned right again onto Main Street. The police station was tucked between a crystals and incense store and a bookstore. As I pulled to the curb across from the station, our pursuers passed us and continued up the street.

They didn't even glance in our direction. Was I being paranoid?

Seth and I exchanged a look. "*Were* they following us?" I asked.

Seth raised a shoulder and let it drop. "Seemed like it."

I waited a few moments and then pulled away from the curb and turned the Jeep toward home. I wasn't going to get Charla or Tom involved yet. What would I tell them? That some sketchy-looking guys followed us into town and then ignored us?

But the incident had left me unsettled.

30

⚘

I sent the kids out back to play with the dogs and called Vi.

She was the one who had gotten me into this predicament. Here I was with a handful of stolen diamonds stashed in my pocket while possibly being followed by mobsters. Now I sounded like Sophie.

I grabbed a sandwich bag out of the drawer and carefully transferred the diamonds into it. I counted ten fairly large diamonds. Just holding them made me nervous. I had to think of a place to hide them. The kids were all over the kitchen like a horde of locusts. They'd surely discover them if I hid the diamonds there. I finally settled on shoving them to the bottom of my box of tampons. I knew Mac and Seth would *never* touch that and Sophie was too young to be interested.

Vi knocked on the front door just as I came down from the upstairs bathroom. She was already talking as I swung the door open.

"I had to ditch your mother and sneak over here," she said. "What's the emergency?" She peered around the living room searching for the source of my urgent call.

I gestured back out onto the front porch. I was feeling trapped in the house with the diamonds and knew the kids would be back inside any minute. After we had settled ourselves on the wicker chairs, I told her about our new clients, Vaughn Jewelry.

"Diamonds!" she said.

I shushed her and glanced up and down the street. Maybe an outdoor meeting wasn't such a good idea.

She rubbed her hands together gleefully. "Even with your ridiculously low percentage, we should earn enough to rent a real office space. That will bring in the customers for sure!" She grabbed my arm and shook it a little bit. "Why did you agree to such a low finder's fee?" She crossed one arm over her chest and rested her other elbow on her hand. She curled her hand under her chin and studied me. "I think I should do the negotiating from now on. Maybe we can write up a standard contract. Rupert can help."

I sighed and studied the ceiling of the porch. "Before you start spending the money, let me finish."

She cocked her head and waited.

"I found some of them."

"Already? That's great." She broke off and put her hand down. "What do you mean 'some' of them?"

I explained the pull to the animal shelter, the search of the premises, and finding a handful of diamonds.

"You're sure you got all of them?" she sat back in her chair and stared out at the street. "Why would the thief split them up like that?"

I shrugged. I had been wondering the same thing. "I'm sure there weren't any more—when I found those, I sensed that was it. I don't think the rest of them were there." I leaned forward, elbows on knees. "If Derek hid them before he was killed, I suppose he might have split them up thinking that if some were found, at least he'd have the rest. If he had them on him when he died, maybe his murderer did the same thing."

Vi tapped a finger to her lips. "Who has access to the shelter?"

"Just about anyone could get in there. They have people coming through all the time to see the animals that are available for adoption. And Francine told me this past weekend had been crazy because the zombie run people came out for tours to see where their charity dollars would go. She made it sound like half the county and their cousins had been through."

Vi grinned at me. "*And* their cousins? That's a lot of people."

I flapped my hand at her, recognized that it was her gesture, and pulled my hand back. It's bad enough when I think I'm becoming my mother, but if I think I'm becoming my aunt, I won't be able to live with myself.

Then I told her about the followers. She grew very quiet.

"I don't like the sound of that," she said. "We can't tell your mother—she'll flip out and try to hire bodyguards or something. Are you sure they were following you?"

I shook my head. "Not sure, but it felt like they were."

"Then they probably were. You need to trust your instincts more. Didn't they teach you that at the police academy?"

"They were more interested in teaching us the law and procedure. There wasn't a lot of focus on psychic intervention."

Vi scowled at me. "I don't mean psychic, just instinct. I'm sure even Mac uses that."

I wasn't sure where she was headed with this, but I didn't want to go along for the ride.

"I'm going to try again in a little while and see if I can locate the other diamonds."

"Let's do it now," she said. She stood and headed toward the house. "Where are the kids?"

"In the backyard with the dogs," I said.

"I'll send them into town to get some ice cream, then we won't be interrupted."

I stopped her at the door. "I don't want them wandering around alone with those guys lurking in town."

"Right, good point." She pushed the door open and stepped inside. We heard the kids in the kitchen, rummaging through the fridge.

I followed Vi to the kitchen. The dogs milled around underfoot, hoping for a crumb or, even better, an all-out spill. Seth had the bread, meat, cheese, condiments, and chips all pulled onto the counter.

He looked up and grinned as we entered. "Hi, Aunt

Vi," he said. "We're starving. Do you guys want a sandwich?" He gestured to the counter and with a practiced hip check shoved Baxter away from the meat. Tuffy was too short to reach the counter, but he leaped high enough to see what was there. Sophie was in the pantry filling the dog bowls with kibble. Both dogs pointedly ignored the food and continued to stare at the sandwich fixings.

"That's a great idea, kids," Vi said. "Let's eat and then Aunt Clyde is going to demonstrate how she finds lost things."

My mouth fell open, and I glared at her.

Sophie bounced on her toes and clapped.

"Wicked." Seth grinned. "Do we need the pendulum?"

"What's a pendulum?" Sophie asked.

Vi turned to her, hands on hips. "Do you mean your mother has never even shown you a pendulum?"

Seth held up a hand, "I'd never seen one before last summer."

Vi narrowed her eyes at him. *"Hmph."*

I stepped into the fray. "We don't need a pendulum for this, but we can show one to Sophie later. Let's eat, and then I guess you guys can help me."

I scowled at Vi and waited my turn at the counter to make a sandwich. I had promised Richard and Aaron that I would keep this a secret. I'd have to make something up.

By the time we had all made and eaten our sandwiches, the kitchen looked like a rugby team had scrummed through it. The dogs kept busy searching for anything that may have dropped and Seth ransacked the pantry for cookies.

"Okay, let's get going," Vi said as she crumpled her napkin and rinsed her plate. "I don't have all day."

We went into the living room and sat around the coffee table. It reminded me of another time Seth and I had done this to help Diana cast a protection spell. This time, I was going to try to use the energy in the room to find the rest of the diamonds.

I turned to Seth, "Logan's dad asked me to find something for him, but I promised I wouldn't tell anyone what it was."

Seth held his hands up. "He's a pretty intense guy. I wouldn't want to break a promise to him, so don't tell me."

"How can we help you find it, if we don't know what we're looking for?" Sophie knelt by the couch and looked underneath. "Did he lose it while he was here?" She sat back on her heels and held up a chew toy, which Tuffy promptly nabbed and began chomping. Baxter's ears went down, but he didn't try to take it from Tuffy.

"No, he didn't lose it here," I said. "He doesn't know where it is. I can sometimes sense where a lost item might be. It's hard to explain, but it's sort of like playing hot and cold. I feel a tug when I'm zeroing in on the place. Obviously, it helps if I have some sense of where to start. I've never tried this before, but a friend of mine told me that using other people's energy will sometimes amplify the signal. Like using an antennae to get a TV picture."

Sophie looked blankly at me.

Seth said, "It's like getting a better Wi-Fi router."

Sophie's eyes lit up. "Oh, I get it."

We held hands in a circle and I closed my eyes. I felt weird. I knew they were all watching me like maybe I'd start speaking another language or something. I opened my eyes. Yup, they were staring.

"I think this will work better if everyone closes their eyes," I said. "You guys are making me nervous with the staring."

I waited until they closed their eyes and then I relaxed. I slowed my breathing and concentrated on the diamonds. I saw the ones I had already hidden upstairs and pushed that image aside. I saw an office with a desk and shelves. There was a large plant in the corner. No idea why I would see that detail. It would be much more helpful if I had an address.

I waited a little longer and then sensed, rather than saw, that this was Aaron Vaughn's office.

I opened my eyes. The other three were watching me. "I told you to keep your eyes closed."

"I was starting to fall asleep," Seth said.

"It freaks me out to sit with my eyes closed," Sophie said. Already she had picked up Vi's phrase. She'd be shouting, "I knew it!" next.

"I had to keep an eye on things," Vi said.

I dropped Sophie's and Seth's hands and they in turn let go of Vi.

"So did you see anything?" Vi asked.

"It was strange," I said. "I think I saw Aaron Vaughn's office."

"Maybe he lost whatever it was in his own office," Sophie said. "I sometime lose things in my room."

I smiled at her. "It's possible. I guess I'll have to go there and see what I can find."

We spent the next hour or so playing cards and discussing where to get takeout for dinner. Vi had gone off on her very important business, promising to go to Aaron's office with me in the morning. If it wasn't for the kids, I would have gone there right away, but I'd promised Sophie we'd stay home that afternoon and I didn't mind the time to mull over what I had already discovered.

Mac was home early and we let him choose the restaurant for takeout. He chose Everyday Grill since we'd just had pizza. The kids went up to Seth's room while we ordered. They had become obsessed with a computer building game.

I sat on the couch with Mac. The house was surprisingly quiet for a few moments.

"I got some interesting news today," he said.

I turned toward him.

"The boat that caught fire belonged to Paul," Mac said. "The police assumed they had just taken it, but the boat was sold two weeks ago."

"They weren't even in town two weeks ago, were they?"

"The former owner said the whole transaction took place online. He got suspicious when the buyer sent him cash and told him to leave the key in the boat this weekend. So he kept watch and saw who took it out. He was the one who called the police when it caught fire. He confirms that they got in the boat."

My voice shook a little when I said, "They had to have

been planning the whole thing. From the moment they got here they were planning to leave the kids and disappear." Part of me still worried that they had actually died in the boat. Rationally I knew that Grace called me at that specific time to let me know she was safe, but still. The evidence they left behind led to one conclusion.

"It looks like it." Mac took my hand. "You're hands are like ice. Are you okay?" He scooted around to look at me more closely.

I pulled my hand away. "I'm just trying to process Grace's unbelievable plan. What if I hadn't agreed to take the kids? Would they still have left them here?"

Mac opened his mouth to say something and stopped. We both heard the kids clambering down the stairs.

"Is dinner here yet?" Seth asked. "I'm starving."

"I'll go pick it up." I stood and snagged the keys from the hook by the door. I needed a few minutes alone.

31

Friday morning I took Seth and Sophie to my mom's for a cookie-baking marathon. Vi had talked Mom into it so Vi and I could go to Aaron's office and return the diamonds I had found at the shelter and snoop for the ones I thought were in Aaron's office.

Vaughn's Jewelry occupied a corner spot in a well-trafficked area of Grand Rapids. Windows wrapped around the building and sparkled in the sunlight. I snagged a parking spot just down the street and we walked past a coffee shop and a clothing store on our way to the corner. Vi pulled open the glass door and we stepped inside. I was dazzled by the chrome and glass with high-intensity lights throughout the store. Shelves of glassware, silver trays, vases, and boxes lined one wall. Rolex, Cartier, Breitling, and Panerai watches occupied the vitrine nearest the door. Other glass cases held gold and silver necklaces, bracelets, and rings. The center island contained only diamonds.

"Good morning," a perky blonde woman said as we walked in. "How can I help you?"

"We're here to see Mr. Vaughn," I said.

"Richard or Aaron?"

"Aaron," I said. Vi and I had debated on whether to turn the jewels over to the older Vaughn, but worried that we wouldn't get into Aaron's office that way.

"I'll see if he's available." She walked back to the customer service desk and opened the half door to reach the hallway behind.

Vi and I strolled along the glassed-in displays, goggling at the pieces inside. I started to think again that I had undercharged them for finding the jewels. There must be millions in inventory just in the display cases.

The salesclerk gestured at us from behind the counter and we followed her down the hallway to Aaron Vaughn's office.

"Hello!" Aaron hurried from behind his desk to shake my hand. He turned to Vi and took her hand as well. "Ms. Greer, it's nice to see you again."

"Hello, Aaron," Vi said.

Aaron closed the door behind us and gestured to the chairs in front of his desk. Vi and I had a plan to get him out of his office so I could snoop, but we'd decided to give him the diamonds we had already found. I couldn't wait to get rid of the things.

He folded his hands on his desk and looked at me. "So have you had success already? I've heard the rumors about you, but I have to say I had no idea you'd find them so fast."

I pulled out the baggie with the diamonds and put it on his desk.

"It's only ten of them, but I feel like they're the ones you're looking for."

He pulled the bag across the desk, placed a black velvet board on top, and dumped the diamonds onto it. He took out a jeweler's loupe and examined them. With one eye squinted over the loupe he said, "Yes. This looks like it's from the batch that was taken. We have serial numbers etched onto them and I'll have one of our experts compare them to the list of the missing gems. Where did you find them?"

I exchanged a glance with Vi. We'd decided it wouldn't hurt to tell him where they were and his reaction might tell us something about what was going on. The fact that I was getting such a strong pull to his office had both of us wondering if he had more to do with the theft than he was letting on. I had even started wondering if he had killed his brother because of the diamonds only to be disappointed that Derek had hidden them before the zombie run. Were they in it together and Aaron had his half stashed right here in his office?

"I found them at the animal shelter," I said. "They were in the back office where volunteers leave their belongings while working at the shelter." I had decided not to tell him they were in Logan's cubby. Until I knew what was going on, I didn't want to cause any further family disruption.

"The animal shelter?" Aaron said. "How did they get there?"

Vi and I shrugged. I was only halfway paying attention to the conversation. I was trying to sense the rest of the diamonds. I got a definite pull from behind me. But other than a large plant, there was nothing there. I had assumed I'd need to rifle through his desk, but that felt as cold as any other place. Every time I tried to imagine them in his desk, or on his shelves, I saw the corner where the plant stood, limply, in the weak electric light.

"Can you verify how many are still missing?" Vi asked. "It will help my niece to find the rest if she has a better idea of what she's looking for."

"Oh, yes," Aaron stood up and scooped the diamonds onto a little tray. "I'll take these to the back and check them against the list. It'll just be a couple of minutes. I can send Julie in with some water or coffee while you wait?"

We both shook our heads. We didn't want Julie and her coffee to interrupt our ransacking of the office.

Aaron stepped out, promising to return shortly.

"Take your time," Vi smiled at him.

The minute he left the room, Vi jumped out of her seat and took up sentry duty.

"Hurry," she said. "Do you have any idea where they are?"

I rushed to the plant and felt around behind it and under it. I was about to dig through the dirt when I got another tug. I looked up and noticed the picture of a boat hanging on the wall above the plant. I turned to see if he had any boats on his desk or books about boats. He had a wooden fishing boat sitting on one of his shelves. I picked it up and shook it, but it didn't make a sound. It also didn't feel right.

I had just set it down when Aaron came back in the room. He had seen me.

"Isn't that a great piece?" he came over and picked it up. "I had a local artist make a replica of my boat. I love to be out on the water. Can't wait to get back out there this summer."

He seemed sincere and not at all suspicious that we had been snooping. If I had a stash of diamonds in my office, I wouldn't leave a psychic finder alone in it. None of this made sense to me. And we still hadn't found the diamonds.

"I wonder if we could take you up on that offer of coffee?" Vi said. She knew I needed another couple of minutes.

"Of course, I'll just call Julie . . ."

Vi held up her hand. "I like to make my own coffee. Just show me where you keep it. I'm very particular about my sugar-to-cream ratio."

"Oh, okay." Aaron led Vi out into the hallway.

I heard her asking him questions about the business, his wife and kids, and his boat. I had to move quickly.

I went back to the picture. It was framed in one of those metal poster frames and I pulled the bottom gently away from the wall and ran my fingers along the inside of the frame. Halfway across I felt a soft, lumpy item. I pulled it out. It was a black velvet draw-string bag similar to the one Vi used to store her pendulum, and exactly like the one I had found at the shelter. I heard Vi talking loudly in the hall. I shoved the bag in my pocket and hurried to sit in my chair. I pulled my phone out and was pretending to check messages when they walked in.

Vi handed me a cup of coffee and I raised an eyebrow at her—our signal that I had found the jewels. I hoped that was what I had found. I had no idea how we would get another chance aside from a full-on break-in. Which would probably land us in jail with all the security cameras they had set up. I had a sudden moment of apprehension—I scanned the corners of the office and the top of the shelves for a security camera but didn't see one. I'd just have to hope that the boss didn't have a camera in his own office.

We sipped our coffee and Aaron continued his one-sided boating conversation until the desk phone interrupted us. Aaron picked it up and had a brief conversation. Vi and I pretended to look everywhere but at Aaron. I was waiting for security to come barging in to accuse me of stealing whatever it was from behind the picture.

Aaron set the phone back in its cradle and smiled.

"The diamonds check out as some of the ones that were taken by my brother. I can't thank you enough."

"You're welcome," I said. "How many are still missing?"

"Twenty," Aaron said. "They will be similar in size and value to the ten you already found. Do you think you can find the rest?"

"I'm very confident I can track down at least some of them."

"Great, my father will be thrilled," Aaron spun his wedding ring on his hand. "I can't tell you how hard it has been on my parents—losing Derek and then discovering he had stolen from the family. My mother doesn't know about that part. She's barely spoken since Derek died and Dad didn't want to upset her further by telling her about the golden boy's fall from grace." He looked at us quickly. "I'm sorry, that was an unfortunate choice of words. I know you're both dealing with your own loss. Grace was so lovely. We were all very fond of her when she and Derek were together."

"We're sorry for your loss as well," I said. "It's hard to lose a sibling, especially so young." I felt like such a fraud. Aaron had truly lost Derek and even if he was a jewel thief and a screwup, he was really dead. Grace was only fake-dead, and I was getting tired of pretending to be upset.

We promised to let him know as soon as we found anything and he showed us back out to the front of the store. I took Vi by the elbow and quickly exited Vaughn Jewelry.

32

❧

The enthusiastic doggy greeting when we entered Mom's house made me worry the dogs were confused by the disrupted routine. Seth gave them treats every day when he came home from school but without the cue of coming home, the dogs got nervous. They were never sure when the treat would come and, in desperation, would appeal to me.

I knew I was right when Baxter shoved his head through the strap of my bag and shoved his face inside. One time he had found a bag of treats in there and he had never forgotten or given up hopes of another jackpot. Once. He roughly pulled away and the strap caught on his collar. This made him panic and he pulled harder. The bag flipped upside down, scattering its contents everywhere. Mom, Seth, and Sophie came into the foyer to see what was causing the melee.

"Baxter, leave it," Seth said. He bent and took my wallet out of Baxter's mouth.

Mom crouched on the floor and began shoving things back in my bag while Sophie held Tuffy back. Seth held the soggy wallet out to me. I took it and wiped it off on my jeans. I turned to put it in my bag and saw Mom reach out and pick up the packet of tea that Neila had given me a week ago. I had forgotten all about it.

Mom held it up in a shaking hand. "Where did you get this?" I could tell by her tone of voice that she knew where I'd gotten it.

I exchanged a nervous glance with Vi.

"I'll take that," Vi said. "It's mine."

Mom snatched her hand away. "Don't lie to me, Violet."

Seth cast a worried look at me and ushered Sophie and the dogs down the hallway and out the back door.

Mom stood slowly and looked at me steadily. "Tell me."

"Neila Whittle gave it to me," I said.

Mom nodded. "I haven't seen one of these in years, but she still folds them up the same way." Mom ran her fingers over the creases. "How long have you been visiting her?"

I felt my shoulders slump. "About six months. She's been helping me with my dreams. Recently we've been working to strengthen my finding skills."

Mom turned to Vi. "I assume this was your doing?"

Vi crossed her arms and clenched her jaw in her stubborn expression.

Mom turned back to me and waited.

"I needed some help to understand my skills and I found out from Vi that Neila could help."

Vi sniffed loudly.

Mom handed me the packet. "You should drink this. I'm sure it will help with whatever you're working on."

"Mom, I didn't tell you because—"

Mom held up her hand. "I know why. Vi told you I wouldn't approve." Mom sighed and gestured toward the living room. "Let's go sit down. I wanted to talk to you about this anyway."

Vi's eyebrows twitched upward, but she relaxed her arms and followed us into the living room.

We sat in uncomfortable silence for a few minutes. Mom took a shaky breath.

"Vi was right," Mom said. "I wouldn't have approved. I was afraid of Neila because of what she predicted a long time ago." Mom dabbed at her eyes. She had morphed from scary to pitiful.

I reached out and took her hand and she didn't pull away.

"Neila told me about her prediction that you would attend a child's funeral," I said.

Mom met my eyes with surprise in her own.

"She told you?"

I nodded.

"I was so frightened that day. I thought if I kept you both away from her that you would be safe, as if *she* was the threat." Mom stared out the window, remembering. "I was convinced it was you she had doomed with her prediction. It's why I was always so careful with you. It drove your father nuts and I think it made Grace jealous. And then you joined the police. I waited every day for the call that you had been killed on duty. He won't admit it, but I think it's why your father started listening to the police scanner."

"Mom, I'm sorry," I said.

"It's not your fault. You were just a little thing at the time. Grace had been there a bunch of times, but Neila didn't warn me until she met you." She spread her hands out, palms up. "It all made sense."

Vi had remained uncharacteristically quiet all this time, but I noticed she had scooted closer to Mom on the couch and had leaned against her just enough. Sort of the way Baxter does when he knows I'm worried about something.

Mom turned toward me and squeezed my hand. "But this is what I wanted to tell you, and I suppose the fact you already know Neila just makes it easier. I attended a funeral for one of my children this week. It's all over. All the years of worrying about a coming disaster and now it's done. And no one has actually died." She smiled then and I saw every worry line on her face convert to smile lines.

"I think Neila will be very happy to hear that you aren't worried anymore," I said.

"Why don't you invite her for dinner? Do you think she could come tonight?"

"I can ask her," I said.

"I knew it," Vi said. "I just knew it would all work out if Clyde trained with Neila."

Mom narrowed her eyes at Vi. "You and I are not quite finished with this."

I chose that moment to join the kids outside.

An hour later, I pulled up to the stop sign to take a left onto my street. I checked for traffic and saw a familiar car outside my house. I pulled my head back as if that would hide me from Aaron Vaughn. Had he discovered I'd snooped in his office? Was he waiting there to confront me about it?

As I watched, he got out of his car and looked quickly up and down the street. He didn't notice my car sitting at the stop sign and instead of turning to go toward my house, he crossed the street to Tatiana's place.

This was interesting. I knew they were acquainted. She was dating Theo, and they had all been at her shop before the race. But what was he doing here, alone, in the middle of the day?

He didn't go to the front door, but looked up and down the street again and then opened the gate and disappeared into the backyard. What was he doing? I had a sudden thought and pulled out my cell phone to text Diana.

Is Tatiana at work right now?

Yes, she's harassing my customers, why?

Just checking. Talk l8r.

I pulled onto my street and parked in my driveway behind Mac's truck. He'd planned to come home early from work. I couldn't see what was happening in the backyard because of the high privacy fence, but I knew from past experience that I could see most of the yard from my bedroom window. I hopped out of my Jeep and took the steps two at a time.

Inside, I told Mac to follow me and ran upstairs to my bedroom.

"What? Why?" Mac said as he climbed the stairs after me.

I looked out the window and gestured at Mac to join me. Tatiana's backyard was empty. I couldn't see the whole thing, so Aaron could still be there, but I suspected he had already gone inside.

"Mac, I have to tell you something."

I told him the whole story about Richard, Aaron, Theo, and the missing diamonds. I described finding some at the shelter. Then I pulled the velvet bag out of my pocket and told him where I found it. We emptied it onto a small tray. Ten diamonds, just like before.

"We have to turn these in," Mac said.

"I agree, but not just yet, Mac," I said. I kept my eye on the house across the street while I put the diamonds back in their bag and stuffed it into my small jewelry box.

Then I told him about Francine's theory that Aaron may have been jealous of Derek because of an affair with Lila. He stood quietly at the window for a moment.

"We'll have to find a way to get the information to

Roy," Mac said. "I'm afraid if you just walk in there and tell them you were hired to psychically find stolen diamonds, he'll politely listen and then shred your interview before you even leave the building. If he doesn't arrest you for stealing them yourself."

"But it's the truth," I said.

"I know it is, but he's not a believer in any of the Crystal Haven offerings and you have a really strong motive to try to move the suspicion away from Grace and Paul." Mac turned away from the window and paced across the room. "Roy has already settled on his narrative. I'll have to think about how to get him to reconsider. The Vaughns are very powerful in Grand Rapids and Roy could just blame the whole thing on people who are dead." Mac rubbed his hands together to demonstrate Roy's sense of completion.

"Well *this* is pretty suspicious," I gestured out the window to where Aaron had still not reappeared.

Mac nodded. "Yes, but probably not enough for Roy."

We waited, and about ten minutes later I saw him moving through the kitchen to the back door. He pulled the door closed, went into the yard, and opened the gate just a crack. He slipped through the gate and walked to his car. Before we knew it, he was gone.

I stepped away from the window. He'd been inside about fifteen minutes. I wanted to know what he had been up to in Tatiana's house when she wasn't home. But I also wanted to know what he was up to now. Was he looking for the diamonds? If he'd gone there to see Tatiana, he would have known within a minute that she wasn't there.

I thought about the velvet bag I'd found in Aaron's office. It had felt the same as the bag with diamonds from the shelter. I supposed it was possible they weren't even part of the original group that had been stolen, but who hides their own inventory behind a picture? How could I tell Aaron that I had found his missing diamonds behind his own poster in his office? I would probably have to go to Richard.

"Are you coming or what?" Mac said, breaking into my thoughts.

"Where?"

"Let's see where he goes," Mac said. He held up his keys.

33

In the end, we took my Jeep as it was behind Mac's truck. I pulled out and headed in the direction Aaron had gone.

"Stay back so he doesn't see you," Mac said.

I glanced at him and smiled. "Don't worry, Vi taught me everything I know about tailing a suspect."

"That's what I'm afraid of."

We followed Aaron out onto Singapore Highway. I figured he was heading back to Grand Rapids and his office, but he pulled off onto the gravel road that led to the animal shelter.

"He'll see us if we follow him," I said to Mac.

He pointed to a clump of trees at the side of the road. "Pull in there and we'll wait."

It was the same spot Flattop and his friend had waited for me the day before.

"What's he doing at the shelter?" Mac asked.

I shrugged. "Logan works there, but he must be in school right now. Maybe he's picking up something. Or stashing more diamonds . . ."

Aaron didn't reappear for at least twenty minutes. I started to worry that we had lost him through some secret back road when his car pulled out onto the highway. He didn't go toward Grand Rapids, but headed back to Crystal Haven. Mac and I ducked as he passed our hiding spot. I waited until he had taken the first curve through the trees and followed.

When Aaron pulled into a gas station I started to feel like this had been a bad idea. The guy was just running errands. I was reminded of the time Vi had followed one of her "suspects" and texted me photos of his grocery bags.

"I agree he acted strangely when he went to Tatiana's house, but now he's just driving around doing normal stuff," Mac said.

"You're right," I said. "Let's just see where he goes next and then we can go home."

Aaron finished pumping gas and hopped back into his Audi. He pulled out onto Main Street and parked a few blocks from the center of town. I drove past his car, found a spot about a block ahead, and parked.

Mac looked through the back window. "He's coming this way. Do you want to talk to him, or pretend you don't see him?"

"Let's just stay in the car and see where he's going."

We hunched down in our seats. I tilted the rearview mirror so I could watch his approach.

"Is he still headed this way?" Mac whispered even though the windows were rolled up and no one was around.

I whispered back. "Yes, but he crossed the street at the corner—he's not likely to notice us."

We watched as Aaron made his way toward the main business section on the other side of the street. He slowed as he approached the garden, looked up and down the street, and ducked in through the gate.

"He went into the memorial garden," I said.

"Let's go," Mac said. He opened his door and waited for me on the sidewalk.

We strolled casually toward the garden, holding hands. The memorial garden took up a prime spot right in the middle of town. It had been a restaurant, and when it burned down many years ago, the owner's wife kept the land and planted a garden. It was stunning in the summer, with rosebushes and pathways through all varieties of flowering bushes. This time of year the forsythia was in exuberant golden bloom.

Mac and I strolled into the gate and then slowed. We walked far enough into the garden that we wouldn't be seen from the street and then Mac ducked down so his head was below the line of tall boxwoods and arborvitae that lined the path.

"Where do you think he went?" Mac asked. He leaned toward me and spoke quietly.

I remembered meeting Tom Andrews here last summer on a different case. I gestured toward the back of the lot where a bench sat, surrounded by shrubbery and well-hidden from the street.

"If he's meeting someone, it will likely be back there," I whispered back.

We made our way quietly toward the back of the lot and stopped when we heard voices.

"Thanks for meeting me like this, Roy," Aaron said.

Mac and I looked at each other, eyebrows raised. Was Aaron meeting Roy Fisk? And why was by-the-book Fisk meeting a possible suspect anywhere but at the police station?

"Well, it is an unusual—" Roy's next words were swallowed by the sound of a truck rumbling past.

Mac and I crept closer. Both men had lowered their voices and though we could hear them talking, we couldn't make out the words. We circled around the path and finally Mac gestured that I should squeeze between two tall evergreens to see if I could get close enough to hear. We both leaned forward, focused on Aaron and Roy.

"What are you two doing?" Tom Andrews whispered practically right in my ear and I jumped, tripped over some vines, and would have fallen on my behind if Mac hadn't caught me.

Once I had my feet under me I turned on Tom. "Why did you sneak up on me like that?" I kept my voice low, but the irritation was clear. My heart raced and I felt wired from the surprise and the near fall.

"I didn't sneak up," Tom said quietly. He gestured for us to move further down the path. "I came here as back up for Detective Fisk. He's meeting with one of the Vaughns, but he wanted me here as a witness in case anything unusual happened. What are *you* doing here?" He reached out and pulled a twig out of my hair.

Tom looked from me to Mac and back again. Mac had been strangely quiet since Tom had arrived and I noticed a distinct pink flush to his cheeks. He stood taller and gave Tom one of his patented scowls, but Tom had grown immune to such tactics over the past year.

We all noticed at the same time that the voices on the other side of the hedge had gone silent.

"Hold on for a moment, Mr. Vaughn," Roy Fisk said.

Mac's eyes got fractionally larger and he grabbed my hand.

"We're just enjoying the garden, Officer Andrews," Mac said in a stiff, loud voice.

Roy Fisk rounded the corner and stopped when he saw us.

"Andrews, I thought I told you to keep the area clear for the next half hour."

"Yes, sir. You did," Tom said. "I was just asking Detective McKenzie and Ms. Fortune to clear the area."

"Hello, Roy," Mac said. "I'm surprised to see you here. Taking a break from the case, are you?"

Roy scowled. "No, I'm working. But you know I can't discuss it with you."

"Sure, of course," Mac said. "We'll just be on our way."

We walked past Roy and I gave Tom a cover-for-me look that I hoped Roy didn't see.

"You two aren't following me, are you?" Roy asked.

Mac stopped and turned slowly back toward Fisk. "You're joking, right? Why would we be following you?"

Roy held his hands up. "Just checking, I know you have an interest in this investigation."

Tom stepped forward. "I'm sure you would have noticed if you were being followed, Detective Fisk."

Roy stood a bit taller. "You're right, Andrews. I'm sure I would have noticed."

Aaron rounded the corner of the path then. "What's going on here? I thought this would be—" He stopped when he saw me. "Clyde? What are you doing here?"

I held up the hand that was clasped in Mac's. "Just out for a stroll. Mac had the afternoon off."

"Oh. I, uh, just needed to get some information from Detective Fisk here." He studied the path and the bushes and looked everywhere but at me. "It seemed too nice a day to meet at the police station."

I nodded at Roy and Tom. And Mac and I turned to continue down the path.

"That was weird," I said when we got back onto the sidewalk and had walked a safe block away from the garden.

"It was," Mac said. "Aaron acted like we'd caught him doing something wrong, and Fisk was twitchy. When the only *normal* person is Andrews, it makes me nervous."

I checked my watch and hurried back to the Jeep. Mac and I rehashed the last hour on our way and came to the same conclusion as before: Aaron was up to something, but we didn't know if it had anything to do with his brother's death. I drove home and pulled into the driveway. Mac said he'd meet me at my mom's for dinner, kissed me, and climbed out of the Jeep. My next mission was a much happier one. I hoped Neila would be willing to forgive my mother.

Even in the past few days, the long driveway to Neila's house had become more colorful. Daffodils and tulips spread along the drive and the dogwoods had already begun to fill in with flowers.

Neila was on her porch when I drove up, shaking out a throw rug.

She handed it to me when I approached and indicated that I should give it a good shake. She had a couple of them lined up and I wondered once again how she always seemed to know when I was on my way.

After all the rugs had been thoroughly shaken and were draped on her porch railing, she invited me inside.

"Did the tea work for you?" she asked.

I snapped my head around to look at her. "I haven't tried it yet, but that's sort of why I'm here."

"Oh?" She gestured toward the kitchen as usual.

"Actually, I can't stay," I said. "I came to see if you'd like to come with me to my mom's house for dinner tonight."

Neila's eyes glistened in the pale evening light. "Rose asked you to invite me?"

"She found the packet of tea and knew it was from you. Once I told her I had been seeing you for the past six months she invited you to dinner."

"Oh, my." Neila looked around her entryway and pulled her shawls closer around her shoulders.

"She's not . . . worried anymore," I said. "We had Grace's funeral this week."

"Yes, I know." She laid a gentle hand on my arm. "I think it will be enough. I only ever saw the funeral, not the actual . . . death."

"So, you know that Grace . . ."

"Isn't dead? Yes."

"But how?"

Neila smiled and slowly closed her eyes. "I think I'd like to just change and then I can come with you. Do you want something to eat while you wait?"

I shook my head no. I wondered if other people felt as weird around me when I made predictions and found things. Because sometimes Neila sort of freaked me out.

34

That evening, dinner was a boisterous affair.

Mom had greeted Neila with a big hug and an apology for all the years she had avoided her. Vi also hugged Neila and there was something about the familiar way they said hello that made me think I wasn't the only visitor to Neila's house in the woods.

Seth had never met Neila and he maneuvered his way to sit next to her. As he quizzed her about her talents, it was the only time I ever saw him leave a plate full of food untouched.

Sophie was less impressed and I think she was jealous of the attention Seth showered on Neila. Mom had made beef stew, which was Dad's favorite, and I wondered if she had plans for him. He had a theory that

Mom made his favorite dish only when she wanted a favor. It was also the recipe that Neila made every fall to remember my grandmother. I saw her eyes well up a bit when Mom placed a bowl in front of her.

Mac happily tucked in to his bowl of unemotionally laden stew and seemed content to let everyone chatter around him. He'd been unusually quiet this evening, but I didn't sense any tension or worry. He was probably ruminating on our afternoon of following Aaron.

"So what do you know, Mac?" Vi leaned past Sophie and me to address Mac.

He placed his spoon next to his bowl and smiled at Vi. "Not much, Vi. What do you know?"

She flapped a hand at him. "Tell us about Derek's investigation."

"I don't think we need to do that right now, Vi," Mom said. She cast a worried glance at Neila and I suddenly realized she wanted to impress her.

"If I wait until after dinner, he'll disappear on me," Vi said. "He's like smoke."

"You shouldn't smoke, Mac," Sophie said seriously. "It's very bad for you. We saw some nasty-looking lungs at school. They were all black and shriveled looking."

Mom's spoon clattered to the table. Vi took Sophie's hand and squeezed it.

"I meant he's hard to pin down," Vi said. "He doesn't actually smoke."

"Oh, good." Sophie smiled and pulled her hand away so she could go back to eating.

"I don't have anything to report, Vi," Mac said. "It's not my case."

Vi narrowed her eyes and sat back in her chair. "And you're telling me that you just happily go about your own business and you haven't asked any questions about the case?"

"You must have heard something, dear," Mom said.

The tension had returned to Mac's shoulders. "They are pursuing multiple leads. I wish I could tell you that they had found the killer, but they haven't."

"Do they still suspect . . ." Dad glanced at Sophie. "The people they suspected before?"

Mac nodded and rubbed his jaw. "I think that will be a top lead unless something else comes along."

The table was silent for a moment, each person working on his or her own interpretation of what Mac said.

"I hate to eat and run," Neila said. "It was delicious, Rose. Just like your mother used to make. But I'm not used to being out and about so late and I'm really quite tired. Mac, would you drive me home?"

I caught the smile that passed between them and knew that Neila was just trying to save him from my family. I had told her how they loved to involve themselves in Mac's cases.

Mac stood so quickly he almost knocked his chair over. "Of course, Ms. Whittle." He walked around the table to her chair and helped her to stand.

"I'll walk you out, Neila," Mom said. "I hope you'll come again."

"Just when I was getting somewhere," Vi muttered to Seth.

* * *

Mac was already home when I returned with the kids. I could tell they were tired due to the lack of arguing when I suggested they should get ready for bed.

I went to the kitchen while they trooped up the stairs. I set the electric kettle to boil and put Neila's tea into an infuser. Both Mom and Neila thought that this would help and I needed it.

I took my mug into the living room where Mac sat staring at the wall opposite.

"What's up with you?" I sat next to him on the couch.

He pressed his lips together. "I'm finding it difficult to stay away from this case."

I gave him a small smile. "Really? I'm shocked."

He grimaced. "I talked to Andrews after you dropped me off. Roy is still focused on the fight with Paul. Andrews didn't know why Roy decided to meet Aaron at the garden instead of the station. And I heard through another contact that Aaron and Derek had been fighting just before the race. So there are multiple witnesses to that fight, just like the one with Paul. I don't know why Fisk is so focused on Paul and Grace. Or how to get him to consider other possibilities."

"We'll think of something," I said. "We don't have any more proof that Aaron or Richard was responsible than they have against Paul. It's all just gossip."

"Yes, but with missing diamonds, now Aaron and Richard have a motive," Mac said.

35

❦

*I am in the alley again with Tatiana. The same alley
I saw in the crystal ball. The pirate zombie is gone
and she has stopped crying. She beckons me forward and leads me through a maze of cardboard boxes
and furniture piled so high I can't see over it. I turn
to try to orient myself, but the pathway behind has
closed off.*

*I turn again and look for Tatiana, but she is gone.
I run ahead to the next turning point and look both
ways. She's disappeared. I choose the right fork, but
only about ten steps along I hit a dead end. I return
to the intersection and take the left side. This leads to
another choice—again there is a dead end or a path
that leads to another branch point.*

It feels as if the piles of boxes and furniture have

been getting progressively taller and more menacing. But I sense that the diamonds are here somewhere, among the boxes. I stop and wait for a hint. There, in the corner. I see three enormous diamonds. I can barely stuff them in my pockets. When I turn back toward the pathway, it has become narrow until I have to turn sideways to squeeze through. I can't turn around because the boxes are closing in behind me.

I look up ahead and see that the path is clear and wide. I move quickly toward the wider opening and just as I step out of my narrow pathway I stop and pull back.

I look down and down and down. The maze has led to a cliff. I feel the familiar dizziness and nausea that accompanies any brush with heights. I push my back against the wall and close my eyes.

Saturday morning I woke with the now familiar fuzzy, groggy, post-dream feeling.

I remembered Aaron sneaking into Tatiana's house and I knew I had to get inside and see if the diamonds were there. I had no clear idea of how the stolen gems were connected to Derek's murder but I was certain they were. Was he killed for the diamonds? Was he killed for another reason that had forced him to steal them in the first place? Did he fight with his brother and the whole thing got out of control?

And if they *were* in Tatiana's house, how did they get there? Did Aaron put them there yesterday, or did he go there looking for them? And what about the knife? Was it the same one Tatiana had purchased from Diana?

I slumped down the stairs in search of coffee. I found Mac and the kids laughing and eating frozen waffles in the kitchen.

"We're going to see alpacas today!" Sophie said. "Seth says they're like llamas and I don't know what those are, either, but I bet they're cute."

I looked at Mac. "Alpacas?"

He swallowed and pushed his empty plate away. "My mother," he said.

That was really all he needed to say. His mother, Lucille, had found a local alpaca farm and was "sponsoring" some alpacas in exchange for their fleece. She had concocted this plan during a recent knitting retreat and had become obsessed with the skittish animals.

"What time?" I asked.

"She wants us over there by eight thirty." Mac stood and kissed my cheek. He leaned forward and whispered. "I told her you were busy."

I mouthed "thank you" and stepped to the counter to slide my own waffle into the toaster. I poured coffee and leaned against the counter.

"Get your shoes on and we'll go," Mac said to the kids.

"You can't come see them, Clyde?" Sophie asked.

"Maybe next time," I said. "You can give me a full report when you get back."

"Okay." Sophie skipped out of the room and I heard her chattering to Seth in the living room.

"You didn't sleep very well," Mac said. It wasn't a question.

I shook my head no. "Just a lot on my mind."

"Take a break and we'll figure this out together," he said. "See you around lunchtime."

The minute they left, I ran up the stairs to peek out my bedroom window at Tatiana's house. I saw her moving around in her kitchen and hoped she planned to go to work. Weekends were the busiest time for the shops and for those with psychic offerings. Mom occasionally worked all day on a Saturday during the summer.

The dogs straggled in and sat with me as I staked out Tatiana's house. Tuffy sat on my foot and stared up at me, probably trying to send me thoughts of dog treats. Baxter leaned against me and rested his chin on the windowsill.

After half an hour of alerting me to every bird and squirrel in the neighborhood, Tuffy and Baxter wandered off in search of more interesting pursuits. I had just decided to quit when Tatiana came out of her front door. She turned to lock up, climbed into her Mustang, and drove away. As I heard the vehicle rumble down the street I realized I could have just listened for her car and saved myself a stiff back and a nagging headache.

I texted Diana and asked her to let me know when Tatiana arrived. A flurry of questions ensued. I dodged them and then received confirmation that Tatiana had settled in for a morning of palm reading. After the bonfire lighting last weekend, she had been quite popular. Everyone likes to try out the new talent.

I went to the kitchen and rifled through my junk

drawer. Finally, after pulling out rubber band balls, screwdrivers, a small hammer, dead pens, and old Chinese food menus, I found what I was looking for—a key with the label MILO'S PLACE attached. I just hoped Tatiana hadn't changed the locks.

I grabbed some stretchy black gloves that were still in the basket by the door from this past winter and went across the street. I pretended to knock while sliding the key in the lock. Seeing my black-gloved hand against the door reminded me of the dream of the funeral. I tamped down a sudden worry that this was a very bad idea. Tatiana was slightly irritating, but not dangerous. The key worked smoothly and I stepped inside.

I had never been in the house. The former owners weren't very friendly and I'd never needed to come in after they left. Milo had given me the key in case of an emergency and I'd never used it.

The layout was classic, with a dining room to the right, living to the left and the kitchen at the back of the house. Tatiana still had boxes piled everywhere. I wove my way through the living room, feeling another brief warning as I remembered last night's dream. But it only confirmed my instinct that I needed to search Tatiana's house. I found that the kitchen had been set up. No boxes here. Also, I was getting zero tugs toward the diamonds. My heart raced and I felt like I was breathing too heavily. I wasn't accustomed to entering someone's house uninvited. I stood still and closed my eyes, concentrating on the diamonds.

Upstairs. I climbed quickly, worried Tatiana would

return any moment even though Diana had said she would let me know if the palm reader left the store.

There were two bedrooms and a bathroom off the landing at the top of the steps. The bathroom felt "cold." One bedroom had been set up and it felt cold as well. The other bedroom was filled with boxes, clothing, and some cast-off furniture. I stood in the doorway, still breathing heavily, when my mind settled on a small roll-top desk. It hid behind a stack of boxes in the far corner of the room. I might not have noticed it if not for the sense that I had found what I was looking for.

Why would Tatiana have some of the diamonds? Did she know Derek better than she had let on? She did appear out of nowhere just as Derek came to town. Then several things clicked at once. Who had access to Aaron's office? Who had I seen at the shelter? And who, besides Tatiana, could have hidden the diamonds here? I suddenly realized that a warning about Tatiana coming home was not what I needed. I needed to get out of here, but I knew I was close to the diamonds. I took a chance. I worked my way past piles of bedding and clothing, stubbed my toe on a headboard that was lying in the middle of the room, and almost knocked a whole stack of boxes to the ground.

I made it to the desk and opened the lid. It slid up with a loud squeak. Inside there were about fifteen small drawers and cubbies. I began opening them in order and found a small velvet bag in the fourth drawer down. I pulled it out.

"I'll take that," said a voice behind me.

I jumped and backed into what I assumed was the barrel of a gun.

I slowly raised my hands and he took the bag from me.

"I'm really sorry, Clyde," he said. "I always liked you, but even as a kid you were too nosy for your own good. You know, Grace got in all sorts of trouble when you told your parents about us smoking. She blamed me since they were my cigarettes. Your parents told her I was a bad influence. Then Derek started calling her and hanging around, charming everyone. Things might have been different if you had kept your mouth shut."

"Theo, you don't have to do this," I said.

He laughed a short bark of amusement.

"Don't tell me what I have to do," he said. "Put your arms down and hold them behind you, slowly."

I did as he said and he pulled off my gloves and slipped a rope around my wrists. "I couldn't believe it when Derek came back to town claiming he was going to move back here and work at the jewelry store. I think he just said that to get at the diamonds."

A few wraps and I felt the knot tighten. He took my phone out of my back pocket and patted me down.

"Come on, Tatiana could be home any minute."

I didn't see the point in arguing with him about Tatiana's whereabouts. He grabbed my upper arm and steered me back out of the room. I stumbled once, but he caught me and I didn't fall.

He pulled the ladder to the attic down out of the ceiling and pushed me toward it. I awkwardly climbed up, leaning against the steps so I wouldn't lose my balance. If he didn't have a gun, I would have pretended to fall and tried to knock him down, but I couldn't chance it with a firearm in the mix.

The attic was warm and dusty. I heard a few squeaks and saw bats hanging in the rafters.

"This place is creepier than I thought," he said, looking around.

He pushed me toward a wooden bench that had been shoved against the wall. He gestured that I should sit and I finally got a good look at him. He was just the same as always. His open, friendly face made me think for a moment that this was all a joke. Then he pulled a roll of duct tape off his arm. He must have snagged it from the room with all the boxes. Tatiana favored a purple plaid design and Theo tore off a strip and covered my mouth.

"I can't have you making any noise up here when T comes home," he said. "Don't worry, she'll see it my way eventually."

He wrapped my ankles with the tape and secured them to the bench leg. He patted my head.

"I'll be back soon," he said. "And no noise. I'd hate to have to use this." He waved the gun and descended the ladder. The trapdoor swung up and I was plunged into a gloomy, dusty, bat-infested prison cell.

36

The minute he was gone, I began working on the rope around my wrists. I had held them as far apart as possible when he tied them. Now I tried to push them closer together to see how much play I had in the rope. Not as much as I had hoped and my shoulders ached from holding my arms behind my back.

I struggled with the ropes and tried to pull my left arm out because it felt the loosest. My watch caught and dug into my arm. Then I tried good old-fashioned wiggling. I hoped the knot wasn't very tight. By twisting my arms and trying to make the knot tighter, I hoped to loosen the rope enough to pull my right arm out.

I heard rumbling in the distance and the engine cut off just outside. Tatiana was home. Theo must have called her. He was probably laughing at the frantic texts from Diana.

My stomach dropped. Diana was the only person who knew I was even paying attention to Tatiana. If Theo answered her from my phone, he could tell her anything and she'd never warn Mac that I was in trouble. Why hadn't I put a passcode on my phone?

"What do you mean, she's in the attic?" I heard Tatiana's angry voice just below the trapdoor. Theo's deeper voice responded, but I couldn't hear what he said. *He* wasn't shouting.

The voices moved away and I continued to work my hands free of the ropes. I felt like I was almost there, but it was very tight. Finally, my right hand slipped free and I pulled my arms to the front, rubbing my shoulders and my wrists.

I pulled the tape carefully off my mouth and listened. It sounded like they were all the way downstairs. Tatiana's voice carried and Theo's was just a low rumble, but I didn't think they were fighting anymore. I didn't know if that was good or bad for me.

My ankles were encased in tape. He really wanted me to stay put. I looked around in the gloom for anything sharp to cut the tape. I felt along the edge and underneath the bench and was rewarded with a sharp puncture to my finger. I had found a nail.

I dug it out with my fingernails until I could just barely grip it and then started working it back and forth to pull it free. It was hard work and I was in a weird position, sprawled on the bench with my ankles tied to one corner. If I could have used both hands at the same time, I could have done it, but I couldn't twist that far.

I stopped every few minutes to listen. It had grown very quiet down there. I hadn't heard the Mustang, so I assumed they were still in the house. I glanced at my watch. It had been two hours since Mac and the kids had left for the alpaca farm. How long could it take to pet a couple of skittish fleece producers? But would Mac even know where to look for me? Diana wouldn't send up an alarm if Theo had answered her text. No one else knew I was here and Mac might not consider looking across the street. He didn't even know I had suspected the diamonds were at Tatiana's house.

No, I had gotten myself into a mess by coming over here alone. I had completely discounted Theo. I was so busy suspecting Tatiana, or Aaron, and so sure that I had her under surveillance that I had been incredibly stupid. If I ever *did* get out of here, Mac would be absolutely justified in any reaction he chose. Mostly I feared his disappointment. We had been such a great team recently. Except for the fiasco with Roy. How would he ever trust me again even if I did get out of this?

All of my ruminating had given me extra energy and I finally pulled the nail free with a loud creak and a broken fingernail.

I went to work on the duct tape. I poked holes along the tape that attached me to the bench and then poked holes between those until I was able to rip free of the bench leg. It happened suddenly and I fell, knocking the bench over with a giant thud. I sat very still, listening.

If Theo had heard, he'd be up here in an instant and all my work would be negated.

I waited through twenty breaths. Then forty. I didn't hear any footsteps thundering toward me. I awkwardly stood and placed the bench gently back on its feet. I sat and began working on cutting my ankles apart the same way I had just cut through the other tape. It was laborious and I think he had wrapped it at least three more times than he'd used to tie me to the bench, because it took a long time to make each hole. My fingers were slick with sweat and the nail kept slipping.

Finally, I pulled the tape off my ankles. I tried to stand, but my feet had the pins and needles of inactivity and odd positioning. I rubbed the feeling back into my ankles and feet and listened again for any sound from downstairs.

I stood carefully and waited for the tingling to pass. There was one small window in the attic with a broken windowpane. That must be the bat family's front door. I stood on tiptoe and rubbed the grime off the glass to look out.

The window faced the backyard, which was surrounded by a high privacy fence. I would have to stand on the bench to see if there was a ledge, or a gutter to use to get to the roof of the back sunporch. What I did know was that the ground was very far away. Just thinking about it made me dizzy.

It wouldn't be safe to try to escape through the house. I was pretty sure Theo and Tatiana were still there, probably plotting my demise. If I were a criminal, I wouldn't leave the house with a hostage inside. The only way out was through the window.

I picked up the bench and placed it carefully under the window. I stepped up onto it and peeked out the window again. There was a small ledge there and I might be able to get to the rain gutter by edging along the narrow overhang. The point of the roof appeared to be about ten feet below the window. I'd have to hang from the gutter and drop onto the steeply pitched roof of the porch. If I didn't fall off at that point, I'd have to figure out how to climb the rest of the way down without slipping or raising the alarm.

I looked at my watch again. Three hours since I had seen Mac. They must have come home by now. Were they already looking for me? Had they texted and Theo responded, so they thought I was safe and on an innocuous errand? I didn't have time to wait to be rescued, I would have to pull myself together and climb onto the roof. The last time I had been up this high I had almost passed out from the panic that set in. I'd keep my eyes straight ahead. I would not look down.

I wrestled with the latch and, with a loud protest, it unlocked the window. The sash was stuck. I pushed and prodded, but didn't want to pound on it or make any noise. I climbed down and searched for a cloth. I'd have to break the glass and climb out through the small and ragged frame.

I didn't see a cloth, but I did find a heavy vase in a box of old junk. I tapped on the glass, thinking it would be less noisy. I managed to crack the glass and then I slipped out of my T-shirt and wrapped my hand in the cloth to clear the shards. I repeated the process with the three remaining panes. Finally, in an all-or-nothing gesture, I swung the vase at the remaining slats. The wood splintered and cracked and I began breaking off the rest of it to make an opening big enough to crawl through. I heard thundering steps from below. Theo shouted something.

I used the vase again to clear the rest of the frame, pulled my shirt back over my head, and tried to hoist my foot up onto the sill. No good—the window was too high. I heard Theo on the landing just below the trapdoor.

"Theo, stop," Tatiana said. "What are you going to do?"

"She's up to something," he said. "You heard the crash."

I didn't have any more time.

"She lives with a policeman," Tatiana said. "Don't hurt her."

I heard the squeak of the ladder unfolding.

"I can handle it," he said.

I jumped up and wiggled the front of my torso onto the sill. I looked down even though I had promised myself I wouldn't. I am eminently untrustable. It was so far down that I'd have to be much more agile and much less dizzy from the height to avoid breaking my neck. I decided to face Theo and see if I could talk him down. I tried to pull myself back into the attic, but I was stuck. Like Winnie-the-Pooh in the stories I used to read to Seth and Sophie, half of me was in and half was out.

I waited for the worst. What was taking Theo so long? I figured he'd have dragged me back inside by now. Then

I heard the most wonderful sound in the world. Sirens. And there were flashing lights in the street below. I twisted to try to look behind me. I heard shouting and a loud thump through the open trapdoor.

"Clyde!" Mac shouted.

"I'm here!"

I felt hands on my hips, lifting me back into the room. I felt the bench beneath my feet and turned to hug Mac. I had never been so glad to see him.

37

⮜⮞

Safe at home, I sat on the couch with Baxter's large head pushing down on my legs as if he was trying to keep me from going anywhere. Diana and Alex had come over immediately after I called them to say I was safe. My family arrived with food and questions.

Mom and Vi bustled through the living room passing out cookies, tea, and lemonade. Mac was still across the street giving a statement to the police. They had agreed to let me come to the station later that afternoon.

When Mac had seen me, covered in dust, with bleeding fingers, red welts on my face from the duct tape, and my shirt inside out, he'd ushered me quickly out of the house. I'd heard Tatiana explaining she knew nothing about me being in the attic until Mac had broken down the front door. Theo cast a menacing look at me from between two police officers, but he wasn't speaking at all.

The front door opened and Mac stepped through and closed it behind him.

"Well," Vi said, "what's the news?"

"They're taking Theo and Tatiana in for questioning." Mac started to push Baxter out of the way and then decided to squeeze next to me on the other side. He took my hand.

"We've been waiting for you, Mac," Dad said. "Seth won't tell us a thing."

Mac raised his eyebrows at Seth. Seth shrugged and looked at the carpet.

"Seth, Sophie, and I went to the alpaca farm with my mom," Mac said. "I got a weird text from Diana asking if Clyde was okay. Seth and I both texted Clyde, but she didn't answer right away and when she did, it didn't sound right. By then, we were already on our way home." Mac held his hand out toward Seth. "You should tell this part."

Seth sighed and seemed to shrink into himself. "Baxter was very worked up when we walked in," Seth said. He glanced at my parents and then at Vi. "I tried to calm him down but he was very clear that we needed to go get Clyde from across the street."

Mom gasped and grabbed her amulet.

"I knew it!" Vi said. "You can hear them. Just like me!"

Mom wiped a tear off her cheek. "Oh, Seth, we're so proud of you."

Vi crossed her arms and pursed her lips. "So just how long has this been going on?"

"Vi, let him tell his story and you can interrogate him later," I said. I still hadn't heard how they figured out so quickly that I was across the street.

"Baxter showed me that he had watched out the window with Clyde for a while in the morning. I saw lots of birds and squirrels, but I knew Clyde was probably not looking at them. Then Baxter said she was across the street and had been most of the morning."

I petted Baxter's head and he looked at me almost as adoringly as Tuffy looked at Seth. Baxter was the hero once again.

"I didn't know about Seth's . . . ability, but I was worried enough about Clyde that I decided to go check," Mac said. "Tatiana answered the door and she acted so nervous I got very suspicious. So I called Tom and Charla and told them I needed backup because I thought Clyde was being held against her will."

"They believed you?" I asked.

Mac shrugged. "They didn't even question it."

Mac gave my family a sterilized version of finding me in the attic, leaving out the fight with Theo at the base of the ladder and the fact that I was stuck in the window. For my mother's sake, he also left out any mention of bats.

My parents and Vi lingered for about an hour more, mostly questioning Seth on his abilities. Alex and Diana left, promising to return later with dinner.

Charla called Mac to fill him in. Tatiana was talking nonstop and Theo had not said a word. Fortunately, he'd told Tatiana enough that they were able to piece together the story.

Derek and Theo had been friends since grade school, with Theo acting as the sidekick to Derek's exploits. Derek thought nothing of stealing girlfriends, taking credit for Theo's successes, and generally walking all over him. Why Theo put up with it was a mystery. But, once Derek left town, Theo was able to start his own very successful career with Vaughn Jewelry. He wove himself into the Vaughn family and felt as if he were another son to Richard.

Then Derek returned. Theo caught him making a pass at Tatiana during the pre-run party at Tatiana's store. Theo was not going to let Derek take anything else away from him, so he lured Derek into the woods and stabbed him. Mac said that he might have been able to claim a crime of passion except for the fact that he had stolen the knife from Tatiana's shop when they all left for the run. When Theo found the diamonds in Derek's pocket, he remembered Aaron and Derek's fight at Tatiana's shop. Theo decided to try to frame Aaron by hiding the diamonds in his son's cubby and in his office. Hiring me to find the diamonds had been Theo's idea. He hoped I would tell the police and implicate Aaron in the theft and the murder.

"But what about the mobsters?" Sophie asked. "Are they still going to follow us around?"

"They've left town already, Sophie," Mac said. "They were also after the diamonds. Derek had promised to turn them over at the zombie run, but Theo got to him first. They didn't know who had killed Derek, so they were keeping an eye on anyone they thought might be involved."

"How did you find all that out?" I asked.

"I ran into them in town and we had a nice, quiet conversation," Mac said.

"So who left that 'threat' on the car for Grace and Paul?" Mom asked.

Mac smiled. "That was Tatiana. She got tired of hearing Theo talk about how wonderful Grace was and how close they had been."

"Does that mean Mom and Dad can come back?" Seth asked.

I shook my head. "I don't think so," I said. "Your parents were worried even before those guys showed up, and they had obviously been planning their disappearance for a long time. I'm not sure how long they will be gone, but you and Sophie will be safe here with Mac and me."

"Do you think we can find Miranda and let her know?" Sophie asked. "She'll be worried about me if I don't come back."

"I already have somebody working on that," Mac said. "We'll find her and you can talk to her on the phone."

Sophie wiped her cheek and smiled at Mac.

38

A few days later, Vi and I sat in our new shop. I read the Grand Rapids newspaper report about Derek's death while Vi pounded on a calculator and muttered to herself.

We had just swept out the last bit of fringe that had been left behind by Tatiana. She'd left town shortly after being released by the police. If I had liked her more, I would have told her that her new notoriety would only help the business. As it was, I was glad to see her go.

The Vaughns had paid the finder's fee on all thirty of the diamonds. I admitted to Aaron that I had seen him sneak into Tatiana's house and had followed him. He'd been there at her request; she'd asked him to appraise some of her jewelry. She said she had wanted to sell some of it and trade in her car, but didn't want Theo to know. She claimed Theo was overprotective and would have tried to buy her a car on his own. He had stopped at the animal shelter to drop off some food and other items for the dogs. It turned out Aaron never would have found the small velvet bag hidden in his office.

With their money, Vi and I were able to rent the small shop next to Diana that Tatiana had vacated. I was surprised at how thrilled I was to see our sign go up out front: FORTUNE SEEKERS.

Sophie had started school and by the second day had met her best friend. I only hoped for her sake that it would work out as well for her as it had for me when I met Diana.

Vi slid her glasses off and let them hang from their beaded chain. She pushed her old-fashioned ledger away and sat back in her chair.

"We're in the black and can even afford some new furniture and a small advertising campaign," she said. "How about we get Seth to paint the walls light gray and we buy a plum-colored velvet couch for the front? Your mom can make us some bright pink and orange throw pillows."

I was only half listening because someone had just slipped a letter through the mail slot. The mail never came so early in the day. I got up from my desk chair and bent to pick up the envelope.

It was addressed to me. There was no stamp or postmark and no return address. I slit the top open with my thumb and pulled out the folded, yellowed piece of paper.

My hand shook as I unfolded it.

A childish rendering of the Eiffel Tower had been drawn on light blue construction paper. It was fragile and had already ripped at the creases. White fluffy clouds and a smiling sun filled the sky. I had drawn this for Grace when I was about Sophie's age. I couldn't believe she had kept it all these years. It could only be from her.

I turned the paper over and read the message.

Thank you.

It was unsigned.

FROM NATIONAL BESTSELLING AUTHOR

DAWN EASTMAN

-The Family Fortune Mysteries-

PALL IN THE FAMILY

BE CAREFUL WHAT YOU WITCH FOR

A FRIGHT TO THE DEATH

AN UNHAPPY MEDIUM

Praise for the Family Fortune Mysteries
"A tightly plotted, character-driven triumph
of a mystery...Eastman is fabulous!"
—Jenn McKinlay, *New York Times* bestselling author
of the Library Lover's Mysteries, the Cupcake Bakery
Mysteries, and the Hat Shop Mysteries

"Filled with eccentric characters, psychics,
and murder...Stellar."
—Kari Lee Townsend, national bestselling author
of the Fortune Teller Mysteries and the
Mind Reader Mysteries

dawneastman.com
facebook.com/dawneastmanauthor
penguin.com